SONG OVER QUIET LAKE

SONG OVER QUIET LAKE

Sarah Felix Burns

Second Story Press

Library and Archives Canada Cataloguing in Publication

Burns, Sarah Felix, 1977-

Song over quiet lake / Sarah Felix Burns.

ISBN 978-1-897187-67-8

1. Indians of North America—Canada—Residential
schools—Fiction. I. Title.

PS8603.U745S65 2009   C813'.6   C2009-904198-7

*Second Story Press gratefully acknowledges the support of the Ontario Arts
Council and the Canada Council for the Arts for our publishing program.
We acknowledge the financial support of the Government of Canada through
the Book Publishing Industry Development Program.*

Published by
SECOND STORY PRESS
20 Maud Street, Suite 401
Toronto, ON M5V 2M5
www.secondstorypress.ca

*This novel is dedicated to all the people
I have known who have lost a child,
or have been lost themselves as a child.
I never knew what to say to you at the time
so I sat down, thought about it for a while,
and wrote you this book.*

PROLOGUE
The Priest

"Here is your soup, Father MacAvoy." Paul, a young postulant, places the shaking soup bowl down on the planked table. Father MacAvoy likes his soup bowls large and filled to the brim lately, though he barely touches the steaming liquid within.

"Thank you, Paul." Father MacAvoy's aging vocal chords convey his frailness. He is now in his nineties, given to being a shut-in most of the time. With considerable effort and some assistance from the novices, he is still able to attend the daily Eucharist.

He will die here, he is sure of it. The Holy Cross Priory in Toronto has been his home for the last seven years. Before his time here, he had been called to many exotic locales to undertake his active orders in service to the poor and less fortunate. In recent years, he has been able to focus solely on his contemplative orders – a crucial part of the monastic life.

He sets his book aside, not really having read any of it at all. These days he finds himself drifting off into strange lands of memory or dream when he is supposed to be reading. But try as he might, he finds he cannot control his mind. He can no longer harness his thoughts the way he did for most of his nine decades. In his very old age, his mind is taking him in another direction altogether, a direction where he does not feel comfortable.

He supposes it began on the day that he was riding on a streetcar along Queen Street in Toronto about a year ago. That was when he could still get around on his own. He had been to a clinic to have some blood work done, and on the return trip a young girl in a brightly colored tuque plunked down beside him. He smiled at her and she grinned widely back at him.

"Hey, are you like, a priest?" she asked, wide-eyed. He was happy that his presence still garnered that kind of reverential reaction from a youngster in this selfish, modern age.

"Yes child, I am a priest – an Anglican priest."

"Technically, I'm not a child. I'm twenty-three."

"Yes, yes." Father MacAvoy smiled and nodded, intrigued, though somewhat wary of her bravado.

"So, is it true that Anglican priests can marry?"

Stunned and slightly flustered by her question, Father MacAvoy cleared his throat and smiled.

"Yes, secular clergy are entitled to marry but members of a religious order – monks like myself – are required to remain celibate."

"Celibate! That means no sex, right? Wow, you lived your whole life with no sex? Oh! I'm sorry! That was a rude question. Sorry. I just never met a priest – or monk – before." She smiled and shrugged and put her mittened hand over her mouth.

Father MacAvoy was at a loss as to how to respond. He had never been approached in such a way before…well that's not entirely true. He had been similarly challenged in the same defiant way years ago. But it was different back then, so many decades before, when the Indian boys in the residential schools teased him about not having sex. Residential schools —

"Residential schools?" the young woman asked. *Had she read his mind? Or worse, had he spoken aloud and not realized it?*

"Do you know about residential schools?" he asked her.

"Yeah, we learned about them in high school." She said flippantly. Father MacAvoy was never quite comfortable about how remnants of his early life had become political fodder these days for liberal school textbooks.

"Oh, and plus my older sister knows this elderly Native woman who was in a residential school," the girl added. "I think it was up in the Yukon – the school she was at."

School in the Yukon. Those were the words that troubled him most. The girl had chattered on about this and that, peppering him with embarrassing questions until she hopped up from her seat at her stop some twenty minutes later. Though Father MacAvoy smiled and waved her off, he had been highly unsettled by her. Something that she had asked about had bothered him deeply, and he was left feeling absolutely raw. That a simple trip on public transport could have left him so exposed was highly bothersome. He had the very strange sensation of being a writhing fish, marooned on shore, drowning in the air, breathless and powerless to get to the water, which was just beyond his reach. He vowed never to take the street-car again. And due to his declining health, he never did. Now, on the rare occasion that he leaves the Priory for medical appointments, a junior novice drives him.

What got him thinking about all this again? Ah yes, the soup. There it sits, steaming and beckoning, before him. He takes a few meager spoonfuls, but leaves the rest. When Paul comes to retrieve the bowl, Father MacAvoy requests the same bowl and the same portion be delivered the following day. *Perhaps tomorrow will be the day.*

And it was.

That next day was the day that Father MacAvoy unwrapped the bottle of red wine he had so carefully stashed away in his tiny closet months before. It was a sin to steal, especially from your own priory's cache of sacramental wine. But what he was about to do was a far greater sin – a mortal sin that would ensure he'd end up in hell and suffer the deprivation of a Christian burial.

His mind would not allow him to relent. After Paul delivers the soup bowl and they exchange their usual greetings, Father MacAvoy watches the novice swoosh out the door for the final time. Once Paul's footsteps can no longer be heard down the long corridor, Father MacAvoy retrieves the bottle of wine and begins drinking it straight from the bottle. He drinks as much as he can, as fast as he can, before gasping and collapsing on the floor. But he fears his plan will not be completely successful unless he can pull himself up to the wooden table where the soup is waiting. He heaves with all of his geriatric might and is able to gather himself up and balance his frail body on the chair, facing the table, and the soup. He lifts the bottle and drinks the remaining wine with no regard to the fact that his throat muscles are not able to keep up with the downpour. Rivers of red wine flow down the sides of his cheeks and neck. When the entire bottle is depleted, it falls from his hand, smashing on the hard floor. He gives pause for several moments to allow the fluid to enter every vein of his body. He becomes weary, even more than he has been in recent days, and his head begins to swim to where there is no up or down, bottom or surface to the water. He is drowning.

When exactly his head had dropped into the large bowl of soup, he does not know for sure. But his lungs fill quickly with the broth and he cannot – will not – lift his head. He gasps for air, but only liquid fills his lungs. Is it wine, or soup, or vomit? It doesn't matter. He is dying.

All is turning to darkness and he thinks that it is the end. But an image appears before his eyes.

A child, a brown female child with shorn hair. Wearing a ruffled uniform with heavy stockings, as though from Victorian times. He recognizes her, he knows her from some-where, some time long ago, but what is her name? What became of her? Where is she now? He cannot remember her name.

She reaches for him, her hand thin and bony. He is para-lyzed, he cannot control his body, he floats and tumbles down, down, into the depths. He finally lands on the bottom. It is very dark down here, black. He cannot see; he cannot breathe or control his body. But he feels something. He can move his hand to feel a face – a little face with glasses. And he feels the large ears on the side of the head. Just a boy. But wait, the boy is sitting upright in something – a chair with wheels.

In an instant, the priest is back in his childhood. He is standing on the edge of a ditch in Dunnville, a small farming community in Ontario, his boyhood home before the First World War. There are children there – young boys, eight or nine years of age. It is the neighborhood gang, up to mischief on a warm sunny day in late winter. The boys often played around the irrigation ditches at all times of the year. But their parents always warned them that the most dangerous time was late winter and early spring because the ice on the ditches could not support their weight and freezing water rushed below the ice. Of course, those stern warnings only made the boys more curious.

And there was little Herman Maloney in his wicker-cane wheelchair with the wooden spoke wheels. It must have been around 1910 when Herman was about six years old. The priest sees himself as a little boy too, all of seven, and he is with the gang as they cajole and lure Herman to the edge of the irrigation ditch. Alex Sumners had told the other boys that if one of them dove into the hole in the ice and floated under the ice in the ditch all the way to the other side of the culvert tunnel, he would give him a dollar. None of the boys volunteered, but they convinced Herman to try it. Herman was what the adults called a "simpleton;" the children just called him "retard." He looked the part with his perpetually crossed eyes behind the thick lenses of his glasses, which magnified every twitch in his face. He could walk, but not very well because his leg muscles were tight and spastic.

The priest stood and watched as the other boys took

Herman's arms and pulled him out of his wheelchair and down the side of the embankment. At first Herman was smiling, willing and eager to be part of their fun. For he was often left out of the games, sitting in some corner or away from the group, watching from under some shade tree. He was gleeful at first when they crowded around him and chanted for him to dive into the hole in the ice. His face was beaming with a large buck-toothed grin, so thrilled he was to be part of the gang for once. One of the bigger boys lunged forward and pushed Herman from behind. In he tumbled, into the freezing March waters of the fast-flowing irrigation ditch. As soon as he entered the water, the smile vanished from Herman's face. He whimpered in panic and clung desperately to the jagged edge of the ice.

"Swim Herman, swim!" the boys chanted. Alex Sumners raised up his boot and stomped on Herman's clawing fingers. In the swiftest instant, Herman was gone, carried away by the rushing waters, pulled under the layer of ice, further on into the ditch. But the ice was clear enough that the priest could see through from his vantage point up on the embankment. He could see little Herman's distorted body being swept helplessly along. He could see the sheer terror on the little boy's drowning face. He could feel it too; but he was frozen; not a muscle would move. His voice was absent, his tongue useless. The power and presence of the group of boys was so burning, he shrank back inside himself. And then Herman was gone. Washed away with the melt-water into the culvert and beyond. Perhaps Herman could have survived if there had been an air hole, a break in the ice on the other side of the culvert. But there wasn't. The gang of boys did not realize this until they had run over to the other side of the culvert to find Herman. But there was no Herman.

In fact, Herman's body was not found until three weeks later – by a farmer some six miles out along the irrigation ditch. The boys had told their parents that Herman had simply fallen from his wheelchair along the steep embankment and tumbled into the water of the ditch. The priest had told the same lie. And a lie that devastating could never be confessed.

At Herman's funeral, all of the boys were present – somber, tight-lipped, miserable. Herman's mother was in the front pew, sobbing. She was a beautiful young thing with long red hair tied back in a single braid.

"My only child! My baby! Why were you taken from me?" she screamed in her grief at the lifeless little body in the white casket.

Her tears were unrestrained. The priest could see how they flowed down her face and drenched her black dress, how they puddled onto the floor. It seemed as though her tears were filling up the entire church with a liquid so heavy it could only be despair. Soon he was drowning in it. Soon he could not breathe again, and was gasping for air. But only the dark liquid filled his lungs.

Then a hand. The little brown hand of the Indian girl. He reached for it, grabbed it, and felt it pull him away from the church, away from the dead boy in the casket, away from the mourning mother.

It was her. Remembering her face from so long ago, he remembered her name.

CHAPTER ONE
Lydie

My name is Lydie Jim. I tell you the story of my long life. I am eighty-two years old and next month I graduate from the University of British Columbia.

Around the year 1915 I was born on a trapline in the area of Quiet Lake in the Yukon, North Canada. Back in those old days it was a long ways walking from Whitehorse, but now riding in a car, it does not take so long. I was the oldest child of my family but I was fourth to be born. The other three older ones – two boys and a girl – died when the camp burnt down and they was buried inside. Then my mum had me born in a lean-to on the trapline while my dad was out cutting rabbits from his snares. In the olden days people lived in bush camps and moved around with the seasons. Then after me, my sister was born on the trapline too. It was during the time that my parents were sick with the epidemic. But they didn't die.

My dad was blind most of his grown-up life because of another sickness – the one they called the measles – it made him go blind when he still was young. But he hunt moose, lynx, muskrat, and caribou and he fish and trap anyways because that's the way things was back then. And he knew how to do it so well he could do it with his eyes closed, he said. But his eyes were always open and he still couldn't see. Daddy was blind and sick and my mum was expecting my sister child and sick with the epidemic in the lean-to on the side of the trapline. It was a very bad time for them and all of the inland Tlingit people that year. I was three years old then and my mum sent me outside to boil water on the fire and cut up rabbit to put in the pot. I fed my mum and my dad the stew because they could not get up on account of the sickness and the big baby in mum's belly. Then, it was time for the baby to come and my mum told me what to do, how to catch the baby when she come out and stick my finger in her mouth to pull the stuff out and then cut the cord with a clean knife, and tie it up – the cord – not the knife. That's how I helped my baby sister be born when I was three years old. My mummy so sick and shaky after that, she couldn't feed the new baby from her breast. My mum tell me to take the rabbit's brains out of its head and boil them up with water – that's what they did back then to feed babies, because it was so soft to eat, full of vitamins, it made the baby full.

I tell you this now so you know how it was back then for my clan of the Tlingit. That was many years ago and things change a lot in my lifetime. I think of us on the side of the trapline now sometimes when I sit in class at university. I am an old lady now. Next month I will get my degree in Women's

Studies. I get to come here for five years now for free, because I am a senior citizen and because I am an Indian. Back in the old days, Indians never got to go to schools like these. Just the residential kind where it was all about religion and discipline. Now the government feels bad, I guess, because of what happened to the Indians back then so they try to recruit old Indians like me go to school at the University of British Columbia. One thousand Indians at UBC by the year 2000 – that's the admissions office goal. They need to get their Indian quota, so they say come Lydie, come to our big fancy school so it looks like we are being nice to the Indians. So I say sure, if it's free, I go. But I think it's funny how they always think the best thing for us Indians is going to school.

It's good here though. I like the spooky old buildings on campus and all the interesting people I meet. And they don't make you eat soap here or none of that other bad stuff like they did when I was young.

Nope, it's all about books and writing papers here. I get to read a lot of books and I learned to write better and the professors love me to tell stories in my papers for sociology and anthropology classes. They give me pretty good marks and tell me to keep telling my stories because they say I am a *treasure chest* of information. Funny thing is, how come if I'm a treasure chest, they don't pay me for my stories? That's okay though, a couple times they put my stories in their journal articles and they say they don't make much money off that so they're not getting rich off my stories either. Not that I want to get rich off my stories. No way. I never want to have lots of money – that makes bad things happen to a person. Look at those rich people on the soap operas – always bad stuff happening to them. I just like to tell my stories so these young people, specially the white ones, can know how different it used to be. And maybe they will figure out that you can live without cordless telephones and those computer things. Maybe. Some of them are pretty far gone though. But that's okay too, 'cause they're still good people. And I know things have to change. Over time, everything changes.

One thing most people don't know about me when they look at me is that I'm part white. My mum was a half-white lady and my dad was full-blood Tlingit. My mum's dad was a white-man prospector during the gold rush in 1898 but he never found no gold so he made a living selling goods inland for the Hudson's Bay Company – that's where he made friends with the Tagish and Tlingit people. His wife was a Tagish Indian girl from around Carcross and they had one baby girl together before the wife died of some disease. Grampa was left alone with a little half-blood girl so he had my mum married off when she was real young – nine or ten – to local Tlingit guy he friends with. That's how she met my dad. She marry my dad young and he was good to her. He never learned to speak English in his whole life, just the language of his clan. That was the language my mum learned too and they spoke it to me until the government workers took me away to residential school where I had to learn English. When I finally was allowed to go back to stay with my mum – my dad was dead by then – I forgot many of the old language and my mum forgot English so we couldn't really talk to each other. After years being around my people again, I picked up the traditional speaking that the residential schools tried so hard to make us lose. Then my mum died too, but at least we got to hold hands and sing again. That's one thing I never forgot was Lydie's Song. The one my mum made for me. It had some words and a pretty tune and we would sing it in our throats over Quiet Lake – so beautiful it made the hairs on my arms tingle. She tell me in her mother's language that everyone should have a song. That's the tradition in the way of my grandmother's people. And she say, she can't give me much but she can give me a song. And that song will always stay with me no matter what happens to me or where I go. And all the time through my life, whenever I hurt alone, feel sad or mad, or even happy and proud, I sing Lydie's Song in my head and I can hear the words float over Quiet Lake and it makes me smile.

Anyway, we burned my mum after she died – in those days they burned dead people – then we had a party for her, like they did when Tagish or Tlingit people die. Since my mum was half Tagish, they brought her bones and ashes back to her mother's clan in a trunk to put them away in the little spirit house at Carcross. That's what they did with dead people back then.

CHAPTER TWO
Sylvia

I have always wished I were someone else. For as long back as my memory can take me, I wanted to have someone else's life. The first person I was, outside of my given identity of Sylvia Hardy, was a girl named Abigail Greenwald. She was the same age as me and she was my earliest friend, notwithstanding the accuracy of the term "friend." When I was just four years old and my younger sister was two, our mother went back to work as a health care aide. We stayed with a babysitter during the day who had two other charges the exact same age as us, Abigail and her younger sister. Our babysitter – Melanie – used to take us over to the Greenwalds' house on the other side of town, or vice versa. And since we were the same ages, we were good at keeping each other occupied and out of Melanie's hair. It worked out well and that was the arrangement for many years, even when we were in school and just needed after-school watching.

The problem was that the Greenwalds were more affluent – from the other side of the tracks, quite literally, in Medicine Hat, Alberta. They first lived in the Parkview neighborhood on the South Saskatchewan River in a large stately home, but then moved to a new subdivision in the early 1980s; the first residential development to be built south of the Trans-Canada Highway. Though their old house was quite grand, a newly constructed home in the newest part of town seemed to be more of a status lift for the up-and-coming professionals of the day. Abigail's father was a lawyer and her mother worked – or was on display – at the cosmetics counter at Sears, so she could show off her perfectly made-up face and designer clothes and shoes. She was very well put together. The whole family was.

My life was somewhat different than Abigail's. My step-dad, Floyd, was perpetually unemployed due to a perceived or real (I still don't know which) chronic "bad back." We were on and off welfare when my mother was between jobs and we lived in a large beat-up, boring old white box of a house that had been handed down to my mother from her parents. Tinged by years of neglect and heavy use, the inside of the house was outdated and gritty with second-hand furnishings and musty brown carpeting. Our house was located in the North Flats, northeast of the CPR marshalling yards and the inner city industrial area. And like the name suggests, nothing much exciting happened there. Floyd had the run of the yard, so it was a mess of half-finished auto fix-up projects and engine junk. Scraps of wood and steel and mechanical parts were strewn about in various dilapidated sheds and piled up on old scaffolding used as shelves for the large ugly junk that working-class men covet.

The Greenwalds' new house was a stunning contrast to the Hardy homestead. In the sprawling, master-planned subdivision, it was a long, brick ranch-style house with landscaping, a swimming pool, and a sauna hut out back. They even had someone who came and mowed their grass in the summer and shovelled their driveway in the winter. Needless to say, I preferred to spend time at the Greenwalds' house, rather than my own embarrassingly cluttered and lackluster place.

Abigail was like a goddess to me. Even her name had a glamorous ring to it. She was absolutely beautiful and had everything, every quality, that I did not. She had a real set of parents, not a "broken family." She had long dark, shiny hair and beautiful skin and she carried herself with such confidence, even at a mere three-feet tall as she was when we first met. When I was around Abigail, I would soak in the visual image of her so that I could remember it exactly when she wasn't there. I would absorb every word she said, her way of speaking, her way of rationalizing, her way of chastising me. And when I was alone in my room, I would become her. I would pretend in my mind that I was Abigail Greenwald and that her hair was actually on my head, her pretty face was actually mine, and her words would make their way out of my mouth in front of my cracked oval mirror.

How messed up is that? The truth of the matter – which I can see now after twenty-some years of retrospect, maturity, and intensive psychotherapy – is that she was a spoiled, mean, manipulative little girl. And I was a very vulnerable child.

One incident ended the pseudo-friendship between Abigail and me. She was over at my house playing Barbie dolls when we were about nine years old. We had a fight over whether Santa Claus was real or not. We both initially agreed that he was actually a real person, but then I started rationalizing that it was probably impossible for one man to go around the entire circumference of the world in one night, even if reindeer really could fly. And besides that, how could he fit down all the chimneys in the world, and what if a house didn't have one, like my next-door neighbors' house? Abigail was incensed.

"My daddy says that Santa is real and only special children believe in him! You just ruined me being a special child! You just made me stop believing in Santa! It's all your fault!"

She was crying hysterically by this point and she grabbed my Barbie doll case and ran and locked herself in the downstairs bathroom in our basement. She was in there for a very long time and I was too scared to even knock on the door. I had really blown it. I crept over and sat on the floor near the door and could hear her doing something vigorously inside but I had no idea what. I felt so helpless there on the floor thinking that Abigail was wrecking something in the bathroom my mother had just re-wallpapered and that I couldn't do anything about it. And that it was probably my fault anyway.

My younger sister, Jessie, finally broke through my agonizing dilemma by demanding that she needed to use the bathroom. And when I told her she couldn't, she went upstairs to tell on me. My mother came down, tapped on the door and asked Abigail if everything was alright. Abigail was still sobbing.

"It's Sylvia's fault! She told me Santa wasn't real!" Abigail screamed as my mother opened the bathroom door. We were all speechless for a moment. My collection of Barbie dolls had all been beheaded, stripped down nude and shoved in the toilet. The only sound was Abigail's whimpering and the toilet's weird gurgling noise, as if it were about to throw-up. Then my mother turned to me.

"What the hell happened down here?" she roared. I was so terrified and felt so utterly immobilized that I could not even whisper a word in my defence.

"It's her fault! It's her fault!" Abigail screeched, pointing at me.

My mother banished us to the backyard while she cleaned up the mess and called Abigail's parents. Abigail got in one more dig once we were alone in the yard.

"You're so ugly and stupid – no wonder your daddy ran out of town the day you were born." Of all the things that Abigail could say or do to me or my Barbies, that comment was the most damaging.

From that point on, Abigail would never speak to me again. At least not directly. She would get other girls at school to run up to me and yell in my face that Abigail was no longer my best friend, that *they* were her best friends and I was a piece of stinky garbage who didn't have a real daddy.

Sylvia Hardy smells like farties! Sylvia Hardy is a 'tard-y! That's what they used to sing behind my back. All the way up until high school graduation. Soon it became the common pastime of east Medicine Hat for anyone under the age of eighteen. Making fun of my big crooked teeth and my saucer green eyes, which looked even bigger behind those huge 1980s-style glasses my mother picked out for me. She also made me wear a yellow cord around the glasses so when some kid whacked me on the back of the head, the glasses wouldn't go flying off. The freckles on my pale skin didn't help matters either.

It did let up for a little while when my little brother Tommy got taken away. But that only lasted a couple of months and some kids even blamed me for what happened to Tommy. It didn't matter to me by then, though. I blamed myself more than anyone, and I was too far gone in my own little world of retreat to care what those cruel kids thought of me. Tommy was my little buddy – my half-brother, just a baby and toddler when I was growing up. I cherished him and his chubby-cheeked giggles. He was a soft pillow in the hard world of childhood. My secret strength. He was probably the only one who ever looked up to me. After he died, I was less than nothing.

Life went on without Tommy. My mother went back to work, my step-dad Floyd sulked around and degenerated into more of a slobby grease monkey, which made me resent him even more. The icing on the frosty cake came when my mother brought in a homeless guy to live with us – Boxcar Huey, we called him. A real live hobo off the streets. He was some sort of transitional object in my mother's grieving process, I guess. My sister and I hated him for moving into Tommy's old room. And he was an easy target – he was always drunk and didn't have much in the way of coherent speech in his old age. He certainly didn't have any teeth. He was more pathetic than Floyd. At least Floyd would backhand us if we got too saucy with him. Huey was defenceless against me and my sister. He was a very frail old man. We tormented him by playing mean tricks on him like putting pins on the couch where he would sit. He *never* reacted, which urged us on even more.

But that's all ancient history now. I hardly think of it anymore. The disgusting men in my early life. The father who left when I was only a baby. The loss of Tommy. Those things are behind me now. Next month I will graduate with a psychology degree from the University of British Columbia.

Jessie and I escaped our stifling home-life when we were in our late teens. Our Auntie Chris in Vancouver said we could come live with her for a while, so we did. It was an escape from our mother as much as anything else, and Auntie Chris understood. She was a good ten years younger than our mother and, like us, left Medicine Hat at a very early age. And maybe because of that, she escaped some of the circumstantial depression and bitterness that has afflicted our mother. Auntie Chris is a cool, single-in-her-late-thirties chick with puffy, frizzed-out blonde hair, which she sometimes wraps in a bandanna. My sister and I stayed at her apartment for a couple of years while Jessie finished up her high school diploma. I fooled around at a community college for a while before I decided to get really serious about school. And Jessie took outdoor recreation at a college in the Lower Mainland then taught skiing and snowboarding up at Whistler. When she got bored with that, she went back to school in Toronto – which is where she is now. Studying how to pull-apart dead bodies. She wants eventually to become a pathologist. That's her thing. That and the tuques she wears summer, spring, winter and fall. She's a bit of a freak-show, a goofball, but I miss her all the time. We still talk on the phone a lot. I'll see her next month when she flies in for my graduation.

After I graduate, I plan on staying in Vancouver. I pay pretty decent rent in the two-bedroom apartment I share with my friend, Mui. She's a poet and a lesbian and has a steady girlfriend so she's gone a lot of the time. Our place is not too far from campus, just a block back from the 99 B-line route between Alma and Macdonald. I hang out with Mui's cat Zurbeenie and play the guitar – mostly folksy stuff, but lately I've been into Jazz. It's the kind of music I would have never heard growing up in the dusty-hole town they call "The Hat" in nowhere eastern Alberta. A town whose biggest claim to fame is the huge reserves of natural gas buried underneath the city – *if you dig a hole and light a match, you'll blow the whole darn town right off the map!* I can't say it was all bad, though. To be fair, I liked some things about The Hat – the rugged valley landscape with dramatic drop-off cliffs and peculiar finger coulees, for one thing. And to east of town, the Cypress Hills. My sister and I would sometimes ride our bikes out there and pretend we were pioneers on horses going over the mysterious rolling hills. We got so into the escapism of it, we thought we would see an Indian running over the hills at any minute. We never did see a real Indian. I guess they were all gone by then.

So, here I am in Vancouver. I like it here – except for all the worms and slugs – so I think I'll stay for a while. I'll stay for the coffee on cold rainy days. And the smell of the ocean and the sight of the back-lounging, shell-cracking sea otters. I'll stay for the sound of the seagulls and the cadence of Punjabi, Mandarin, and Cantonese. And for the Thai food, the curry, the dim sum, and couscous. (I had never even heard of those things before I came to Vancouver.) I relish the trips down to Granville Island, the pubs, the micro-brew beer, and the colorful street musicians. The little green guys that live in the redwood trees. Just kidding. There are no little green guys, but there should be – like leprechauns or trolls or something – because Vancouver is that quirky. I'll stay for now, even though the mildew has just about overtaken my basement apartment.

I work part-time at a psych lab on campus, signing up university students to participate in titillatingly bizarre experiments for which they get a very small stipend. I get paid substantially more than the guinea-pig students since I have a "research assistant" position. Psychology is my thing. It has really helped me come a long way in terms of understanding identity formation and sense of self. Also, I wear glasses that are more hip now – retro thick dark frames. And those annoying childhood freckles have faded too. The braces my grandpa paid for helped with the teeth problem. (Now *ya won't look like a Bucky Buckwheat no more!*) The unsightly, garish red hair has been transformed to a deep burgundy, almost purple hue, which I think suits the new me much better. I have it cut in a trendy down-sweep: short in the back and longer straight sides that hug my face – it's all full of the attitude I'd been craving in my early life. My eyes are also much more mysterious, hidden as they are beneath dark black eyeliner and mascara, offset by my pasty white skin. The look may be considered Goth by some, but I think it's more on the upper end of Goth: downtown Vancouver chic. *West Coast womyn.* Due to these up-grades, I have been slightly more socially successful than in the past when Abigail Greenwald ruled my life.

My partner's name is River. I met him in my second year at university. We have been a "couple" ever since. I suppose he was the final element of my transformation journey into *hip urban chick,* since he is all things Vancouver and trendy West Coast. His parents were those ideological hippy types who resided in a communal yurt and some acreage on the west side of Vancouver Island. They own a house in Victoria now and are both university professors. But back in the day, they were apparently quite into the peace and free-love movement. River has five siblings: Sunshine, Moon, Willow, Meadow, and Agate. Agate got the raw deal with that name. Apparently the parents were on a worshipping colorful-mineral-formations kick at the time. Poor Agate. River fancies himself a child of the Sixties, even though he wasn't born until the tail-end of the movement in the 1970s – when things were wrapping up and the hippies were returning to their office jobs and university campuses. River couldn't possibly remember much of life on the commune – he was three when the utopian dream was coming to an end and his family begrudgingly returned to society in the big city of Victoria. But he says it is the ideology that has stayed with him over the years.

I spend a lot of time with River and our group of friends. River is an anthropology-sociology major. He sings and plays acoustic guitar for a little folk band. That's what he does for a living: live gigs around the Lower Mainland at trendy pubs and coffee houses. Sometimes he reads poetry that he has written. But he doesn't get paid for that. His parents fund his schooling costs: tuition, books and all that. They are a close family. River lives with his three older sisters in a rented house in Kitsilano. They go jogging together, do groceries together, and cook together. Which is a little co-dependent if you ask me. But they are open-minded, healthy-lifestyle kind of people. And the sisters are the kind of girls who are extraordinarily beautiful but so unpretentious that they have no idea how they are perceived.

River and I hang out at his place, or mine, at school, Broadway cafes, Jericho Beach, or Robson Street. We also go to the downtown art gallery on free admission day and walk around lower Granville Street buying handmade wooden dolls and carvings from the homeless Native guys who set up on the sidewalks there. River is really into those things – the dolls. He collects them. He says he feels a "connection" with the Native dudes he buys the dolls from. Whatever, I say, you're a white guy who just happened to be born on a commune – what would you know about life on the streets? River is a Rastafarian, so he thinks that is a point of connection. He's always looking for those – points of connections.

That is my current manifestation of a life, in a nutshell. Vancouver, River, Mui, Zurbeenie the cat, Auntie Chris, and Jessie over in Toronto. It's just a little life, but fairly decent on the whole. Oh, and then there is Lydie.

CHAPTER THREE
Lydie

Sylvia's a good person but I get the tickle that she doesn't think so all of the time. I met her in Women's Literature class last year. I saw her there for a few weeks before I introduced myself. She sit up at the front of the class, close to the professor and be really into the conversation the class was having. Sometimes the talk got heated when some of the girls would have a disagreement and Sylvia would get red in the face if someone said something she didn't like. She wave her hand and say, *whatever floats your boat* or some funny thing. Even though I could tell she was still mad. But she try to pretend like nothing really bother her. That's what she try to do.

I like the way her haircut looks. The edges so neat, it's like a statue. She sure is interesting to look at. I saw her name was on a list of tutors from the Resource Center so one day after class I come from my seat in behind of the class and ask her if she be my tutor. She smile and look at me and say, sure.

She got all troubled and flustered about the paperwork and forms to fill out for the Resource Center but I say, we worry about it later. Let's go walking and talking. We walk across campus and down the trail to the beach and sit on some logs. We talk about class and school and her boyfriend with the name River. I tell her about my dead husband, Rooney, and my two sons, Mitchell and Jonah. The boys have white man's names because they born in the time after traditional names fell away. Rooney had a Tlingit name, but he such a poo-poo, I only ever call him by his white-man name.

Since five years ago I live with Jonah. Mitchell's been in prison. Jonah and I got a little place on east side of Vancouver. Old house, yes, but keeps the rain out so 'tis good. Mitchell calls when he needs money for toothpaste or something. He been in Matsqui Institution over at Abbotsford for almost six years now. A few more to go – depends on if he's a good boy. He doing time for manslaughter. Killed a guy up north. Makes me sad to think of what happened up there and now my baby in prison. But I still have Jonah with me. Jonah is a good boy – my youngest. He fixes cars in a mechanic shop and helps with the rent and groceries. No girlfriend for a long time after the last one broke his heart and ran off with their baby.

Lucky thing, neither one of my boys is like their dad, Rooney. He was a mean old man – that's what I called him – Old Man. I never called him mean to his face, but that's what he was. He was twenty-two years older than me. Good thing about that is that he died a lot earlier than me. He hit me and the kids all the time and drunk all the time. Mean old man. I didn't want to marry Rooney but that was the way it was back then after my first husband died. Samuel Jim was my sweetheart from when I was a girl. He was Rooney's younger brother. We married after I left residential school when I was sixteen and he was twenty. We had good hearts together but he died in the war over the ocean. I never wanted him to go because we had a little baby girl together, Gracie, but Samuel wanted to go and show that he still was a warrior, like the old ways of the people, like the tradition so many young Native men wanted to do. He never made it back across the ocean. Died in the first year of the long war. The policemen brought me the letter that told me so. Sad time, but probably good thing because our little girl drownded while her daddy was gone and so now they are together as spirits.

The elders said Samuel's older brother Rooney would marry me 'cause his wife died too, years before. People died a lot in those days. Rooney's kids were already growed so I didn't have to raise them, just my own two sons that I had with Rooney. Mitchell was born in the year 1947 and no more kids came after that so I thought my body dried up. Then, when I was forty-one years old, Jonah came along – boy was that a surprise! Doctors in Whitehorse thought he'd be retarded or something but he was just fine. Old Man said Jonah look like a runt but Old Man never lived long enough to see Jonah grow into a strong young man.

Old Man died when I was forty-four. Good thing for me, 'cause then I could do what I wanted. Bad thing for me was that I had some troubles with the government social workers in Yukon Territory at that time when I was widowed. Those social workers didn't like that I had no flush toilet, electric refrigerator, running water, or separate bedrooms for my kids.

Bad times, bad times those years when the government took my boys away. But I had some cousins in Prince George, British Columbia, so I went down the highway years later with my two boys to go live there. I got a job as a clerk in a smoke shop, do some babysitting, and me and my boys lived there in that small town. Then they both left home and moved to Vancouver. I followed them there – just to see what the big city was like and to be closer to my boys. After Mitchell finish court and get sent to Matsqui Institution, I fell down the stairs and break my hip so Jonah move in with me. He's a good boy, Jonah. Mitchell too, just doesn't know it.

A show on the television last night had me thinking about how it is to be a man in this world. Differences between men and women and all that. Lots of debating about that at the university too. But I think of it another way. Maybe because of the culture I'm from. Women are important to my people, because folks appreciate what they bring. But even now, especially now, it seems to me that women have a strength about them that men never had. And I wonder how did men always get portrayed in the movies and such as the strong ones? How did it come to be that women are made to look like the weak ones who need protectin'? Truth is, it's men who need the protectin'. Really they do. Women have the strong thing inside of them and they can get through anything. They just can. They used to pain of child birthing – pain no man knows – and some women being battered around and not treated right through all the centuries and having to learn at a real young age how to stay alive on the inside when the outside is being hurt real bad. Most all women know that. But men. Those poor men. They just don't have the inside strength that the women do. It's harder for men to feel pain. Rips my heart out to see it in their eyes. And you can always see it.

That's why my boys need me more than I need them. They think I am an old craggy lady, batty in the brain. And maybe they right. But it's important that I knit them winter socks to keep them warm from the cold rainy days. It's important that I still be their mum. 'Cause they need me.

CHAPTER FOUR
Sylvia

Lydie is deliciously funny. She babbles on and tells stories in a round-about way and repeats herself. I can never tell if she is just in the early stages of senility or if she's doing these things on purpose. Maybe it's because she's an old lady, or because of where and how she grew up, or maybe it's because she's just, well, Lydie.

One of the first issues I had to resolve with Lydie was a boundary thing. I suspect that I'm hyper-aware of boundaries because I'm a psychology major. So I had to set limits on the relationship up front. Lydie told me on the second day of tutoring that she wanted to see what I looked like without makeup and glasses. I was appalled by her nerve, if not completely offended, but I had to keep it cool – after all, I was getting paid to spend time with her.

I told her: "Look, we are here to go over the assignments and anything personal isn't appropriate to talk about." I really hate using that stiff word – "appropriate" – but the fledgling professional in me tossed it forth in an attempt at being authoritative. Lydie just smiled and nodded at me.

That first year we were together, things started out a little complicated, even awkward. I guess I can understand, her being a Native elder and all. Having to sit and listen to some young person tell her how to write papers and stuff. And it was hard for me because I knew what I was supposed to do – the Student Resource Center outlined it very clearly in the training sessions and in the handbook for tutors: *strictly professional relationship only*, no hanging out after school, and so on. But as much as I felt bound by the rules, I knew that they weren't going to work for Lydie and me. There was something about her, something about our relationship that made me feel like I could leave my official self behind at the door. Like I could let go of those cultivated things that I tried so hard to be and just not even think about being at all. Because the fakeness felt so stupid around Lydie. With her, I was someone else entirely, someone who giggled and burped out loud. And perhaps because of that, it was impossible to impose the rigid boundaries and guidelines on the relationship between Lydie and me.

At first we would meet at the Crane Library on campus. The Resource Center had dibs on study rooms at Crane but we always seemed to come at the wrong times because the rooms were already full or reserved. Usually we ended up just sitting at one of the long tables in the library's common area. But that was a problem because I couldn't keep Lydie focused on the schoolwork in front of us. She was always watching the patrons coming and going and she was very easily distracted. One day there was a young man with a visual impairment sitting across from us using his fingers to read a book in Braille. Lydie stared and stared at him and I kept trying to redirect her.

"I can feel you staring at me." The young man said pointedly to Lydie. "What is your problem? You never saw a blind person before?"

"No silly. My daddy was blinded so I know all about blind people. You got your T-shirt on inside-out. That's why I look at you. You should fix it and then no one stare."

"I'll wear my shirt any damn way I please," the man snapped as he banged his book shut and huffed out of the room, his metal stick clanking the way out in front of him.

Lydie leaned over to me and said in a not-so-quiet whisper, "These young people today wear their clothes all weird and funny. I can never tell if it's on purpose or by accident."

After that episode, we met in an upstairs storage room at Crane for a couple of sessions, but that didn't work out too well either. Lydie said it bothered her that there were no windows, and the dust from all the old boxes made me sneeze incessantly. We finally gave up trying to do it by the rule book about a half a year in and began meeting at Lydie's place or mine.

I wasn't the expert. That became evident fairly early on. Lydie had a way of teaching while she was supposedly learning, a way of imparting knowledge while I was supposedly the knowledgeable one. Once I let go of the rigid role expectation, something much more comfortable settled in between us. Just softly drifting down from the sky...it was something that you might even call a friendship.

Lydie has lots of wrinkles on her face. Scrunched-up old

lady wrinkles. And I like to stare at her wrinkles, get lost in the folds of them and wonder what is hiding in between each and every one. She looks back at me with laughter in her eyes when she sees me doing this, like she knows what I am thinking – and she loves it. Lydie doesn't keep secrets or mysteries. But she is mystical in her own way.

Eventually, at the beginning of this school year, I quit the paying job with the Resource Center and took on more hours at the psychology lab as a research assistant to make up the difference. I still met with Lydie but it seemed wrong to accept money for it. We had gone beyond the tutor/student relationship. I wouldn't say that we are best friends, but I do look up to her and she asks me for advice – even though I know she always knows the answer beforehand. Now I look forward to our time together, even if it's just going grocery shopping or throwing pebbles down at the beach. It is always good to see her squinty-eyed smile and watch her short wavy hair bob up and down as she giggles at the silly juvenile jokes she cracks.

Sometimes we just sew. Lydie was surprised and delighted to learn that I could sew, so we spend a lot of time sitting on her sofa or my futon just sewing by hand, or with the old sewing machine she has. We've made pillows and small quilts and even simple-pattern clothes that we donate to charity. It is good to spend time with her. I don't know what it is that makes me feel good about our relationship, but I know that it's good.

On this drizzly Vancouver day, I am hopping off the bus a block from Lydie's house. It is refreshing to gasp fresh air after being cramped up in that crowded, stinky, damp bus for so long. It is about an hour one-way from campus to Lydie's house, but that is a normal commute by Vancouver standards. My breath is visible in the moist air and I shiver inside my raincoat. The worms are out all over the sidewalks. I hate walking through Lydie's neighborhood because there are always vicious-looking hungry dogs roaming around at large, sniffing the worms, and shady-looking characters hustling along on foot checking me out like they're trying to decide whether or not I'm worth rolling. Not that I'm fearful, just a little more self-conscious here. Lydie's house is a dump too, old and ramshackle, but she keeps it neat on the inside with her pink and turquoise blue doilies placed ever-so caringly on the armrests of the dilapidated furniture.

When I walk up the overgrown path to Lydie's front door, I see Jonah, Lydie's grown son, standing outside smoking. He nods a greeting to me and looks away.

"How come you're smoking outside?" I ask.

"Lydie won't let me smoke in the house no more. Says it makes her clothes stink." He's talking slowly and he smells like alcohol. Apart from that, there is indeed another stink about him. Something…mechanic-y, like he has been working under a rusty car all week and has not showered. *Yuck. Same smell as my step-dad Floyd.*

"Well, she's right. Smoking's a disgusting habit. I used to smoke. Since I was fifteen, but my boyfriend convinced me to stop a couple of years ago."

"Yeah? He wears the pants, eh?" Jonah smirks at me, then takes a long drink from the beer bottle that was on the railing beside him. He is so casual and barely looks me in the face, as though he's preoccupied with watching television. But he's not. He's facing the street.

"Wears the pants? No, that's not accurate. No, River just, he...well, he cares about health issues and he convinced me that smoking was more damaging than it was enjoyable."

"Sure girl. He's your man."

I hate when Jonah pokes at me like that. He always knows the soft spots to go for.

"Is your mom inside?"

"No. She's at the hairdresser. Getting curls put in or something."

"Huh." I sit down on the rusted old metal chair across from Jonah on the porch. He leans against the railing, his arms crossed over his dirty T-shirt.

"I'm going back to the Yukon soon." Jonah tells me, perking up a little from his haziness.

"You are? For a visit? Is Lydie going?"

"For a visit. And no, she don't want to come. Not yet. Says she has to wait for Mitch to get out of prison before she goes back there. But I been thinking I should go. I haven't been back since we left there as kids."

I am momentarily intrigued by even this little show of something personal from Jonah. It's the most I've gotten out of him in the two years I've known him. Usually he just teases me.

"Shit, Jonah. I mean, that's good that you are going back. Back to your roots I suppose. Are you thinking of moving up there?"

"Don't know. Won't be staying here in Vancouver forever. I got some options. Lydie's okay here, she's got friends and relatives. She's going to move in with her younger cousin Isobel and her husband. This summer, after she's done school. They'll take care of her good. She won't need me here no more."

"What's so wrong with Vancouver? I like it. A hell of a lot more enlightened than the shit-hole in Alberta where I grew up."

"Yeah well, you'll get over it."

This pisses me off. Who the fuck was he? This long-haired, boozy Native guy whose hands are blackened from cigarettes and engine grease and who still lives with his mother? Then I had to laugh when I saw the little smile on Jonah's face. He knows what he's doing. He knows where my buttons are and when to push them.

"Sure Jonah. Whatever."

"I'm going up next month. To Whitehorse. You should come with me," he adds out of nowhere.

His smiling invitation startles me away from my defensive posture. Probably the reaction he was aiming for.

"The night sky up there, all the stars, and the lakes, so many rivers up there…beautiful. Not full of pollution like Vancouver." Jonah draws a picture of the scene he is envisioning in the air with his cigarette hand. "You should come."

"Um, no. Thanks bud, but no thanks. What, are you on some sentimental journey, some vision quest or something?" Oops – that was mean. But I know Jonah can take it.

His eyes narrow at me for the briefest second. Then again, he averts his eyes and exhales from the cigarette. He's a patient guy. Beer in one hand, cigarette in the other. Watching that invisible television across the street again.

"Quiet Lake pulling at your ancestral heartstrings?" I poke at him some more. We do this to each other. He smiles and nods his head.

"It's a fucking campground now. Did my mom tell you that?"

"No she didn't. That sucks, I'm sorry to hear that." I pat him on the shoulder.

"It's a special place up there – 'round Quiet Lake. I remember when we were kids what it was like. Probably doesn't even look the same any more. Some good memories from when I was real young. Hard to tell, though, if they're real or just my imagination doing some wishful thinking. It was a long time ago that I left."

I like it when Jonah reveals these little gems to me. He comes off as such a hard-ass bad dude, but I get the feeling he is a softy underneath.

"I feel that way about the past too. Memories of when I was really young – and I wonder if they are actually real memories or things that I have made up over the years. The further on time gets, the more surreal the past seems, don't you think?"

"Yeah, unless you are an old bird like Lydie who can remember every detail from yesteryear like it was a movie or something."

As he is speaking, Lydie is rounding the corner of the block and then dawdles her way up the front path, patting her shiny new hairdo under her red umbrella. Her hair is still quite dark, despite her being in her eighties. I wonder if she colors it. She's told me no before. But how long can your hair stay black?

"Oh hello Sylvia girl, Jonah. Nice weather out eh?" She giggles her signature Lydie laugh. Jonah nods and winks at me then flicks his butted cigarette out into the cedar brush and hops over the railing to gun up his motorcycle. A moment later he speeds off down the street. My eyes are drawn to follow him. What *is* it about that guy that piques my interest?

On the night bus home I can see myself in the window. The reflection isn't smiling. Once when I was younger, I watched a beauty contest at the local mall in Medicine Hat. The contestants were all dolled-up with thick pink and purple 1980s-era makeup and frilly dresses that made the girls look like dwarfed Barbie dolls. I was standing over to the side where I could see the backstage area – where they would dress and undress, get touched-up by their mothers. I remember seeing that a couple of the girls were standing there in their underpants crying because their mothers were scolding them. A lot of pressure to live up to, no doubt. But the odd thing was that when they entered the stage area through the curtain, clad in their lavish mini-gowns, they were *always* smiling. Big, bright, painted-on smiles that looked like they were frozen on their plastic faces. Even when they lost the contest, or got runner-up, they kept that silly smile plastered on their jaws. It must have been strenuous to keep that up.

At the time I remember thinking that even though it would be hard to do, I would trade anything to be one of those pretty girls. Instead of the red-headed, geeky, skinny girl with homemade clothes whom everyone picked on at school. I would take their lives, with all the pitfalls, rather than mine. Then I got to thinking that trading lives would mean I would have a different mother, different sister and brother. On the way home, I told my mom what I thought about and she reassured me that I was prettier than any little Barbie doll, and Tommy and Jessie thought so too. Apart from all the mean teasing at school, my siblings were my refuge. At home, Tommy looked up to me and Jessie was my playmate, and being the oldest daughter, I was my mom's special helper. Still, there was always that wish, that desire to be someone else, somewhere else.

How does a person get to be who they are? How did me on the inside get this particular skin, this particular body and look on the outside? Apart from the great existential mystery, it took me years to get me to like myself on the outside, though it took some physical manipulation in the form of hairdo experiments, makeup, and so forth for me to feel even close to normal, whatever that is. There is this one girl on campus who is really deformed. She has some type of rare dwarfism disease that makes her very small and her skin looks like it's made out of pizza and sliding off her face, like a zombie in a B-movie horror flick. It's hard to look at her, so usually I pretend not to see her. Other people stare and point and whisper. But she doesn't seem to mind either way. She just goes about her business and seems to have a lot of friends. She's always happy. *How does that happen?* And a pretty girl cries.

The reflection I see of myself looks tired. Like I have been thinking about this useless stuff for far too long. My mother always told me that when you have children, everything changes. You no longer obsess about yourself as an egocentric individual. Instead, everything shifts and begins to revolve around your child, whether you like it or not. My mother lived by that belief in the early years. She always struggled with depression, but she tried hard to overcome it and to be good to us. After Tommy was taken, it all changed. She did this sad kind of retreat back into herself. It felt like she was sliding backwards, away from us – me especially. She did some selfish things after that, like drinking too much, not coming to our school plays so she could go to bingo, forgetting our birthdays, not being there emotionally, not caring.

Before the downward spiral, I used to ask her if I could ever be in a beauty pageant, or be a figure skater or a gymnast in the Olympics. She always stroked my hair and said, of course, I was a gorgeous, smart, and talented person. And she would kiss my forehead and smile warmly, proud of me just for being me. After Tommy was taken, I couldn't ask her any questions like that for a long time, years. Then, one time when I asked her to sew me a dress for the high school fashion show, she told me that I would embarrass myself unless I hid my braces with a closed mouth and got a suntan because I was too pale and thin.

I didn't go to the fashion show that year. I stayed home and wondered if the first twelve years of my life were all a big lie. And that the truth of the world was everything that happened after Tommy was taken.

CHAPTER FIVE
Lydie

An old bitty lady get on the bus sometimes. She is even older than me – I can tell because she is all hunched over, more than me, and boy oh boy is she cranky! She gets on in the Kerrisdale rich neighborhood on the way to school and gets off at the supermarket. And every time she get on the bus she do the same thing. She walk up to some person and say in a high-pitch, whiny English voice: You're in my seat, you need to move! And usually the person is so surprised that they move – not like they would argue back, I mean, she an old woman. She uses her old womanhood and her uppity English accent to always get the seat she want. Even if there a near empty bus and twenty other seats available, she will walk up to some poor person and tell them to move. And usually they do.

One time a young man told her: Fuck-off! She was real shocked by that. She went and tattled to the bus driver that the young man was *verbally assaulting* her and the bus driver pulled over and walked back and told the man to get off or he'd call the police. After the young man stomp off the bus, the old lady turned around and told another person across the aisle to get out of her seat! She crazy, that old bat.

Today I see her get on at her regular spot in front of a block of big fancy houses behind fences made of high, leafy green hedges. Not my lucky day today because she heads right for my seat.

Excuse me, she say in her squeaky English accent, you are in my seat and you need to move.

I pretend like I didn't hear her and look straight ahead. No way is this old bat getting my seat. I need it as much as she does. And I don't give up so easily like those young folks.

The old lady leans in closer and I can smell her flowery perfume, but it doesn't cover how stinky she is. That old lady smell I'm always trying to get rid of. Like she's rotting away under her purple dress and thick stinky stockings.

Excuse me, but you have to move because this is my seat, she say again. She is right in my face so I can't pretend to ignore her anymore. I pat my hand on my ear and nod my head so maybe she believe that I'm deaf.

Are you deaf and dumb woman? She squawks in my face, spitting little pellets of dribble as she talks. I put my hands up in the air like I am shrugging.

You poor thing, she say, you probably can't speak English because you are an Indian aren't you? Nothing sadder than an old Indian lady who can't speak English, you poor dear.

The smelly old lady in the fancy dress sits down beside me. She plumps her shiny sequin spotted purse down on her lap and turns to face me.

the next day, all the time checking the sides of the trail for any sign of cousin. When we get home to Teslin, bad weather set in. Winter came fast that year. It snow and blizzard for three weeks straight so the old trail was covered up and we had to wait until the new snow hardened to go out on the trapline again. My uncles wanted to have a funeral ceremony for cousin but my auntie wouldn't even talk about it. She said she keep dreaming than her son was still alive. We just think she crazy – crazy with grief. Every night she happy to go to sleep 'cause she said she would see her boy in her dreams.

Month and a half later, cousin hobble out of the bush. Cousin! we all said, you must be a ghost! You died out there in the bush. Didn't grizzly eat you? He tired and skinny but he laugh and said he didn't die. The dogs pulled him off the trail that day and he broke loose but must have passed out from the pain of his foot. He woke up, he tell us, and have no idea where he was. He knew his foot was broken and cut bad so he make a shelter with pine boughs and dug into the snow for a cave. He had some dried meat with him and he dug up some scrubby plants under the fall snow so he ate that and drank snow water for first few days. He undid his boot and pant on the bad foot and let it freeze so he couldn't feel it no more. Then he said it was a black stump after four days so then he could walk on it. He made a weapon out of a heavy stick and throw it at a rabbits to kill for food. He said he ate the leather hide from his boot too. He had some matches on him to build fires for warmth and cooking dead rabbits. Fire kept the wolves and grizzlies away too. Then he made some rough snowshoes out of twigs and the left-over boot and rabbit rawhide he twined. People made their own back then so it wasn't like magic. Cousin knew no one was coming to find him so he had to find his own way home. He tried every night to dream the map to get home. He follow the trail he dream in his sleep, just a little bit every day. But the more hungrier and cold and tired he got, the more he dream the map. The fuzzy map home got more and more clear, he said, 'till it lead him right to the road to Teslin.

We all take turns knocking our knuckles on cousin's hard foot – it was black like a bronze statue, and made a sound like that too. Doctors in Whitehorse had to take most of his leg off from the hip down. But he survived.

Elders say it was auntie who showed cousin the way home in his dreams. Elders say that if we listen hard enough, we can feel the ancestors, even the long dead ones, and they will power us, stand with us and show us the way. After cousin came home, I never worry about being lost no more. 'Cause I know now the maps are in our heads. Just like the songs and the stories. We humans go away from our maps and forget the way, but if we dream hard enough, the maps come back.

CHAPTER SIX
The Priest

.

Father MacAvoy drowned for a full three minutes in his soup before his involuntary reflexes or some seizure activity lurched him back and onto the floor. He is lying there now. He is lost in the world of the unconscious – the haunting subconscious that now takes over his mind completely. When he was drowning in the soup bowl, he had come across a little Indian girl. He remembered her name. It was Lydie.

Lydie was twelve years old when she came to live at the school. Choutla School in Carcross, Yukon. She was older than most of the other students who had arrived around the ages of seven or eight. But Lydie was very small and skinny for her age so she appeared to be younger than she actually was. She could not speak English at the age of twelve, only her native language. Father MacAvoy, as her English literature, writing, and composition teacher, could tell that she had a love for learning. He could see something in her that set her apart. The brightness in her eyes. Her eagerness to help. Her heartfelt appreciation when being helped. She took great joy in the act of learning something new. She was fascinated with books. She savored every new word she could add to her fledgling English vocabulary. She gulped up new sounds and sights like she was gulping for air. By the end of her first year at the Choutla School, she was his star pupil and she was nearly fluent in the English language.

To get her to that point, Father MacAvoy had to spend a lot of extra time tutoring Lydie. She stayed after class and was more than eager to put in additional time on lessons and rewriting compositions. He even loaned her some of his own personal books from his private collection, such as *The Adventures of Sherlock Holmes* and *Tess of the d'Urbervilles*. He would spend time reading to her until she could pick out words herself. Eventually, she was reading full chapters to him. He loved the sound of her voice – both joyful and pleasant, innocent yet chiding. He would spend hours with her, listening to her read, watching her face take on the expressions of the characters she described.

He spent enough time with Lydie to raise the eyebrows of his colleagues at the school, but he knew the headmaster would never or could never chastise him for taking an interest in a student. For Father MacAvoy's interest was purely innocent, unlike some of the other known indiscretions of staff at the school. Father MacAvoy could never even think of touching Lydie in that way. He loved her, but as a father. He needed to protect her.

And she brought something to his life that he never had, never even knew existed. It was the knowledge that goodness could exist even in the savage conditions in which she was raised in her early life. It was the knowledge that her soul was as strong and clear as his, maybe even more so, and she had never even been baptized. She personified grace and redemption.

One day a little over two years after Lydie had come to Choutla School, Father MacAvoy was on a spring walk, enjoying the solitude of the chirping birds and the pristine wilderness just beyond the school grounds. He followed a trail and was alarmed to hear the voices of children down an embankment, by a small pond. His instinct was correct: when he peeked over the embankment, he recognized the children – by way of their uniforms – as residents of the school. They were not permitted to leave the school campus, but they had somehow managed to slip away from the monitor's watchful eye during a recess break. The students, perhaps five or six of them, were of both genders and in their early teenage years. These two observations alarmed the priest greatly. Father MacAvoy immediately recognized Lydie among them, her face glowing with delight as she skidded her way across the frozen pond, coming to land face first in the snowbank at the edge closest to him. She did not see him watching her.

The students took turns, but Lydie, being the boldest, skated out the farthest onto the pond. The students were not aware of it, but from his vantage point up above, Father MacAvoy could see that the ice was cracking under their weight. When it was Lydie's turn, she took a running jump start and slid out as far as her lean body would go onto the ice. Panic rose in Father MacAvoy's throat.

"You there! Stop! Stop this at once!" he yelled out over the pond to the students. The ones on the shore looked startled and fled immediately into the bush or back down the trail toward the school campus. Lydie skidded back across the ice as Father MacAvoy stumbled down the embankment to assist her. She made it to the shore, just as the ice began to give way in large chunks, sloshing cold water to the surface.

"Lydie, you could have fallen through the ice!" the priest exclaimed between deep breaths.

Lydie was surprised by his stern voice.

"I can swim Father MacAvoy, and the water's not that cold. I've been swimming earlier in the year than this."

"Lydie, not another word from you. I shall keep this incident from the headmaster's attention but you must promise me – *promise me* – that you will never do such a dangerous act again. Give me your word."

"My word, Father. I will not do it again."

"Now run along with the rest of the children, Lydie." Father MacAvoy shooed her on up the trail and she took off running, so full of life she was.

But he was shaken. So shaken that his breath was still uneven as he sat at his desk to prepare for his afternoon lesson. The students filed in silently, as they always did. But out of the corner of his eye he saw one approach him and put a hand on his elbow.

"It's alright, Father MacAvoy. We're fine," Lydie said while bobbing her head up and down and grinning. He felt the warmth of her hand through the material of his sleeve. She lingered for only a moment, smiling at him reassuringly, then she took her seat with the rest of the students.

He loved her. He loved her in a way that he had not ever

loved a female, even his mother. It was all very confusing, troubling. He looked forward to her voice and seeing her bright smile every day. But this alarmed him. For he knew she was an innocent, and her admiration for him was pure. His feelings for her hovered somewhere in the territory of the damned. They disturbed Father MacAvoy deeply. Because it could ruin her, and most certainly, it would ruin him. The next week he asked for a transfer to a Vancouver parish. It was granted within a month.

CHAPTER SEVEN
Sylvia

There was this bridge down across Hoagies' field, about a fifteen-minute bike ride from our house in Medicine Hat. It was on the outskirts of town, rural land, and there was no actual river but a deep, dry gully that ran under the bridge. The gully filled up with water when the winter snow melted away every spring and it pooled in a sort-of temporary pond under the bridge across the way in Hoagies' field. My sister and I used to go down there when we were kids to play in the makeshift pond. I shouldn't say "play in", because that's not really how it was. We would play *around* the pond, but never actually in it. No way. We were pretty freaked-out about what was in the pond. The melt water was quite clear and you could see right down to the floor of the pond – about three or four feet deep. And always on one end of the pond, there was this massive nest of worms clumped together on the bottom. I guess that's where they hibernated. Sure enough, every year when we'd go back, there was this huge tangle of colorless worms. It actually looked like a big plate of spaghetti because they were so white from being under the snow and water all winter long.

Anyway, we used to go down to the pond under the bridge with Floyd's dog Josie. We considered her Floyd's dog because he brought her home one day and she was kind of gross – always slobby and stinky. I don't think that dog ever had a bath in her life. And dumb. Shit, was she dumb. She always had this big goofy smile on her face with missing teeth and her tongue hanging out the side – saliva dripping down in frothy shoelace trails. She used to chase flies around and around, and even though she never got close to catching one, she would always do it – sometimes for hours. I think it eventually gave her brain damage from the centrifugal force it exerted on her small brain inside that big skull. One time when we were helping out a buddy of Floyd's, hauling hay north of town, Josie jumped up on the back of the trailer and climbed right up on top of the towering stacks of hay. She thought that was pretty cool, but when the hay truck was lumbering down the side of the highway, a huge transport rocketed past and blew Josie right off the hay stack. We yelled, "Where's Josie?" and we looked back and there she was galloping down the road behind us, all banged up and that big stupid smile still plastered on her face. Another incidence of brain damage.

Late one winter, it must have been March or April, Josie went missing. She just wandered off and didn't come back. Floyd used to chain her out in the side yard for the first few years we had her. But then eventually, like many things with

Floyd, that fell by the wayside and Josie was left to wander around the neighborhood with all the other mangy mutts.

The week she went missing, my sister and Floyd and I drove all over Medicine Hat in his pickup truck searching for Josie. Floyd gave up pretty easily saying only that it was one less mouth he'd have to feed. (Not that he did the feeding – he couldn't really cook and he didn't really work – my mother did all that.) But Jessie and I continued to search for Josie. We felt sorry for her. We conducted a circular pattern search like we had seen the search and rescue men do on television – radiating out from our house in North Flats and the neighborhoods beyond. We even snuck into the railroad marshalling yards one evening and ran up and down the tracks looking for a piece of fur or any signs that Josie had met her doom there. We searched the banks of the South Saskatchewan River and all around the industrial warehouses, but found nothing. Eventually, we made it out to the pond beneath the bridge over in Hoagies' field. And there she was.

We saw a matted mess of soaked brown fur caught in some ice on the edge of the pond. On closer inspection, we could tell that it was Josie. Although half frozen, the body's head was turned upward and the mouth was partially open with that big stupid tongue still hanging out, as though she was a taxidermied wolf or something. The sight of her was really horrifying, but worse was the feeling of anger that developed in my gut.

"How could she be so stupid?" I snapped at the cold air over the pond. Josie was probably running carelessly across the thin ice and fell in. She didn't know how to swim either.

Jessie was fascinated with the body and wanted to go get Floyd to take Josie out. But I told her no, that wasn't the right thing to do. We should just leave her there since that is where she died. Besides, the body was beginning to really decompose and smell. Still, Jessie was mesmerized by the way the eyes were sunken in and the body slumped in such an oddly contorted shape, as though it had no skeleton. I pulled Jessie away by the arm that day. But both of us were drawn back there again and again that spring and on into the summer to silently watch the macabre progression of Josie's decomposition.

By mid-summer, the pond under the bridge had dried up and Josie's body, or what was left of it, was now on solid ground. Carnivorous animals were then able to pick at Josie and take whatever was worth salvaging for nutrients, not fat, because she was always thin and bony. Soon, her coat was ripped off in shreds and by fall, her bones were showing. That next winter she was all covered with snow so we couldn't go see her. But when we returned in the springtime when the snow-melt water was just filling up in the pond again, we could see that she was all but bones, picked clean and drenched brown from the dirty melting winter snow.

We went back a few more times after that. Then the following summer was the summer that Tommy disappeared in Calgary. With all the chaos and traumatic emotions surrounding his disappearance, my sister and I thought it best to stay away from the pond under the bridge. Eventually Tommy's body was found up north. And we never went back to the pond again.

Lydie once told me that bones remain as long as the person who they belonged to is remembered by someone alive. Then, when all of those people have passed away and there is no one left who remembers the person, enough time has passed for the bones to disappear. "*Disintegrate*," I corrected Lydie, and she said, "No, disappear." She explained to me about the spirit houses up north and how her people would keep the bones of their ancestors there until the bones disappeared and only stories about the people were left. But no one alive actually knew the person in the flesh because they had been alive so long ago, a time no one today can even remember. The ancestors became like ghosts, living only in story and legend.

I often wonder if Josie's bones are still visible down in the pond under the bridge at Hoagies' field, with the disgusting pile of spaghetti worms.

Last day of class for my History of Slavery course and we all shuffle out with a feeling of relief – though tempered by trepidation for the upcoming exam. River, who is also in the class, walks with me to the bus loop on campus. We stand silent and bored, not noticing much around us, like tired students do at the end of the day. Then we board the bus when it pulls up. Since it is late in the day the bus is full, but not packed like it is in the mornings.

River and I sit on the side seats near the back and I can't help but notice a young mother with two very cute kids bopping around her. They are both little boys and they smile and wave at me. I smile back and make some funny faces, which, of course, the little boys love.

"I really want to have kids some day," I remark to River.

"Really? That's...that's nice, Sylvia." River's response sounds so hollow that even he seems to realize it and subsequently turns his head away from me.

"River, what was that about? You said that like I'd be the worst mother in the world."

"No of course not. It's just that I think you should really deal with some...issues first before you launch into the journey of parenthood."

"Well I didn't mean I wanted to go and get knocked-up tomorrow, or even next year," I say defensively. "I can't believe you would say something so condescending to me."

"It's not condescending. I care about your well-being and I respect that you may want to parent in the future, but I just think you need to do some more work on yourself before you have a small human being totally dependent on you."

"Are you saying you don't think I could handle it?"

"No, no Sylvia. It's just that...well, you do have some mother issues – you admit it yourself – then there is all the stuff about Tommy."

"What *stuff?!*" I ask incredulously.

"Sylvia, relax. We don't have to have this conversation on a public bus. Save it for a more appropriate time and venue." River smiles to the people around us who are now staring at me, awaiting my response.

"Why did you have to go and bring up Tommy? That's just cruel. Are you insinuating that I am somehow to blame for what happened to him?" I rage at River who is now facing me but leaning away, as though I might lunge for his throat. And I just might do that.

"No, Sylvia. But I get the feeling that you still really

blame yourself and I just think you need to maybe get some more professional help before you approach the idea of having children of your own."

I am incensed now. I don't know if I can contain myself. But I am aware of the two youngsters across from me. If I make a huge tantrum scene or deck River in the mouth, I will only be proving his point.

"River," my voice is measured and restrained, "I have endured over ten years of therapy with five different professionals. I think I've had my fill. I think I did my time. There is only so far you can go in therapy, and then life has to go on in its own way."

"You're right, Sylvia. It's a silly thing to discuss. It's all hypothetical anyway. Let's let it go – there, it's flying away now." River gives me a side-hug – as if that will tie up this discussion in a nice, neat bow.

The words "silly" and "hypothetical" really sting me, though. To the point where my anger traps me in a pouty, silent corner. In the nicest possible way, River had just proven his point and put me in a time-out. He was good at that.

That night at River's house, he went on to other things, like what corny movie we should rent and what kind of wine we should drink. River was being overly attentive to me; I, on the other hand, was cold and distant with him. I think he deserved at least that. But the topic of my wanting children was not brought up by either one of us again that night. We had come to an uneasy truce, for the moment. I repeatedly picked up this sewing project – a dress I had been working on for months – trying to do some delicate stitching, but my fingers fumbled and quaked with the needle and thread. Exasperated with my lack of progress, I crumpled the thing up and threw it and my sewing box back in my duffle bag. I had originally planned on giving it as a gift to Mui. But what the fuck – I am so childish and selfish, I may as well just keep it for myself.

CHAPTER EIGHT
River

She is an incredibly restless sleeper. Sylvia tosses and turns and jerks around violently in her sleep as though she is very angry with someone or something. I'll ask her about it in the morning, but typically when she awakens she has no memory of her night demons and she cannot recall what her dreams were even about. At one point, I purchased this second-hand book for her that interprets dreams, hoping perhaps it would trigger some memory or recognition. But she always maintains she cannot remember what went on for her during the night. I watch her a lot like this, when she doesn't know it. I study her movements and her facial expressions as she tries to open a bottle of wine or when she is deep into a book or bored silly from slogging through some journal article. There is a lot a person can learn from watching others closely.

We met at school when I struck up a conversation with her because her posture intrigued me – the way she sat so straight with her hands clasped tightly together. And if she thought someone was watching her – like me. Then she would suddenly become self-conscious and slouch down ever so slightly in her seat. At first she was aloof and untrusting of me, but when she learned I was a musician, it seemed to open something up for her. We went back to my place, grabbed my guitar case and headed for Jericho Beach. I played on the guitar and sang for her while the waves lapped on the shore under a cool evening sky. She had only one song request: *The Boxer.* That one I knew well as a Simon and Garfunkel staple of live acoustic performance, so I obliged with a mellow and nostalgic version. It must have stirred her up because she began to sing along with me. She knew every word. And everything else between us followed in the natural course of time.

Our early dates went something like this: a dinner at a sushi place downtown, a visit to the public market down on Granville Island, ice cream or pastries and cappuccino on Commercial Drive, a walk on Wreck Beach admiring the otherwise homeless nudist dwellers who have thrown all sense of inhibition into the ocean and live probably as human beings were meant to live. If our classes finished up at the same time on school days, we would sit for hours just talking. We would lounge on the retaining walls of the award-winning rose garden situated on top of an underground garage full of miles of concrete tunnels and carbon-emitting automobiles. We bonded in our shared disdain for the architects and campus planners who would think up such a hideous concoction, rather than implementing more bike trails on university endowment lands. We connected in our disgust of the conspicuous consumption habits of Vancouver's affluent

population. And the absurd number of luxury vehicles clog-
ging the streets of the city. I always believed that Sylvia and
I had a strongly shared sense of social justice and environ-
mental responsibility. But over the last year I have detected a
slow shift within her, or perhaps something that maybe was
or wasn't there all along.

Early on she was captivated by my upbringing on
Vancouver Island on a commune the size of her primary
school. She would ask cautious but thoughtful questions
about the sharing of sexual partners and the effect it had
on the children. She was curious about communal parenting and if each child felt bonded in the end with their own
individual parents or just with the community as a whole. I
would explain all of these things to her and she would nod
and tighten her mouth into a puckered smile. She seemed to
lose her sense of conversation after my lengthy descriptions
and explanations and she would always grow quiet, instead
taking on some great interest in the pattern of bronzed leaves
swept up against the curb as we walked across campus. When
I asked her if I'd said too much, she'd always say no, it was
just that she was from a very different world than me. And
she had a hard time reconciling how my parents could go
from utopian hippies to bourgeoisie university professors. I
agree with her that it seems an uneasy and ironic paradox, but
life is full of those, and that is very true of her life as well.

She likes to touch but does not like to *be* touched. She
tells me she is itching to rake a comb through my dreaded
hair, which has not actually been combed for five years now.
She marvels at the way the hairs almost fuse into a mesh of
cotton-like substance and I explain to her that this is the way

hair was meant to look in the natural scheme of things – not all coiffed and shiny and pumped up like a synthetic work of computer-generated art. She tells me that maybe *au natural* was a good fit for early *man*, but she is quite certain that even cave women gave a rat's ass about knots in their hair. When I challenge her about her consumer, capitalist-driven obsession with deodorants, makeup, hair spray, conditioner and all of the toxic chemicals she is rinsing away into the environment, the only comeback she can throw at me is that at least people aren't afraid to sit beside her on the bus. And so our ribbing has gone on with each other for the last couple of years.

The room she calls her own in the small basement apartment she shares with a friend is cozy and clean upon first glance. But the closer one looks, the more dirt and hidden clutter one can find. That was one of the first things I noticed about Sylvia. She tries hard to cultivate this very polished image of herself, but upon inspecting a little deeper, there is chaos and innate insecurity just below the surface. I find this intriguing about her and when I pointed out my observation of her life, she told me I was "too anal for words to describe." She said you can't always tell the inner workings of a person just by studying their domain – there are far too many variables in that. Like not having enough money to pay for a cleaning lady. She does have a valid point, but still, even she will admit that there is more to her than the persona she likes to put forth to the world.

In the summers, Sylvia rushes around panicking to get a job and spends the rest of her time catching up on the television shows she has missed during the school year and going to Star Wars drinking parties or WWF wrestling matches with her subversive female friends. I spend my days slowing down – as one should do in the summer – playing sets with musicians I admire at pubs, hanging out at Wreck Beach with the friends I've made who call it their home. They fascinate me, these people who have left everything of the civilised world behind, though it is so close (the university campus is only just steps away). They raise their children and their weed there on the beach and in the cedars that surround it and nobody bothers them. In fact, I've seen an on-duty cop or two stop by to test their wares. Loosely known as The Wreckers for the name of the beach they inhabit, they are, in the very purest and most stripped-down sense, the epitome of free human beings. And that is what we all strive for, isn't it? In some ways, I think they are the lucky ones.

Sylvia goes down to Wreck Beach with me sometimes but she never stays long because she gets hungry and refuses to buy hotdogs from the regular vendor who "dishes out wieners with no regard to the ketchup and mustard splashed on his own limp but large wiener." And she says it makes her uncomfortable to watch the "obnoxious" professors and graduate students – male – who "go down there and *pleasure themselves* facing the ocean as though the world is entitled to them and their spectacular phalluses." But I tell her that masturbation is only a natural expression of one's sexuality and how did we evolve anyway into such a fickle, censored world where something so natural and beautiful has become taboo and dirty?

Sylvia often responds to my philosophising with something puerile and pointed like: "There you are, there you are doing it again!" And when I ask doing what, she says, "being an elitist West Coast fruity nut," which cracks us both up. I egg her about her eating habits, which consist of far too much dairy, sodium, saturated and trans-fat and she tells me she doesn't need to eat granola because she osmosizes enough of it just by being around me. I point out that "osmosizes" probably is not even a word and she degenerates to "Shut-up, you geek."

Age has never been an issue between us though sometimes Sylvia strikes me as a child in need of much learning and growing, even though she is technically two years my senior. But there are quiet times when I get the feeling that her spirit may be older than her immature demeanor. Like when she sits perfectly still except for her hands expertly working the needle and thread she so artfully moves through fabric, just as her great-great grandmothers must have done before her. And when she comes to see me play live on stage, she sits a few tables back so she can get the full effect of the music and I see this faraway look in her eyes, especially when the blue grass music wraps around her like a memory from back home on the prairies (which she rarely openly discusses with me). And when she sees a child, or when a child comes running up to her to retrieve a runaway ball or to inquire about the bright shiny boots she is wearing. Sylvia's verdant eyes glass over and a gentleness settles in about her that I don't see in her interactions with adults. In the adult world, she can be brash and sarcastic, but with children she becomes something like them – shy and uncertain, wanting to be friends – almost wishing she could run off with them. But she never can because she has passed out of that stage in life and moved on to a crueller, harder reality.

The day after the awkward conversation on the bus, Sylvia left my house early, before my sisters awoke. She says she feels like a third-wheel oddity around my sisters. She said she feels uncomfortable being the only non-family member amongst us. I told her she is family; that when around us, she is one of us and is more than welcome. She shook her head and said, "No, I have not really belonged to a family for a long, long time. Chasing it maybe, but not really having that sense of belonging. I'm the little girl lost. I'm sure you've heard of her."

And off she went on the bus to wherever her broken mind was taking her. I have tried calling her since then, but I keep getting her answering machine or a hesitant Mui saying she is not sure where Sylvia is. I have the strong sense that I need to sit down with Sylvia and have a serious discussion about our future. She does tend to spiral off into the darkside if left unchecked.

The day of our final history exam, Sylvia relents and joins me for coffee on campus. After some discussion about the gruelling essay test we have just completed, I dive into the reason I wanted to talk with her.

"I was thinking, I feel like it is time for us to move in together – take the next step."

Sylvia is quiet. Her only response is to sip the foam off the mochaccino she is drinking.

"You mentioned your lease with Mui is coming due at the end of this school year and you said yourself that you haven't started looking for a new place. Maybe this ambivalence is because you are unsure about where our relationship is going?"

"I really haven't given it much thought – I mean, where I am going to live in two months. I am just trying to get through this exam period and finish up my final papers."

"Well, let me formally invite you to come live with me then."

After a pause with downcast eyes, Sylvia responds.

"Why would you think I would want to move in with you and your sisters? That would make our relationship a little crowded, don't you think?"

"I could get another place – I'm not locked into a lease with my sisters. I could get a place for you and me."

"I don't know River. That's a big step and things have been going fine with our separate living arrangements. Why do you want to go in such a traditional direction? That's not like you."

"Oh, I'm not traditional – you know that. I am just worried that you have no place to go and you will be floating around aimlessly after school is done." Poor choice of words on my part. Sylvia's white skin turned red very quickly.

"Are you worried about dating a homeless woman? I thought those were your people," she scoffs.

I knew this proposition would take a delicate approach, but I didn't think she would get this defensive so quickly. "Look, I think it would really help things. I think it would be good for you to be with another human being rather than holed up by yourself. Interaction, conversation over the morning newspaper…"

Sylvia rolls her eyes. "River, this will probably sound offensive, but what makes you think I would want to move in with you?"

"Because I am your life partner? Why *wouldn't* you want to move in with me? It's an honest question." This seems to soften her a bit. She exhales deeply.

"It just makes me somewhat cagey, to be honest. Nothing to do with you personally – well, no, maybe it is you. I guess I just keep getting the feeling that you are trying to stage an intervention in my life. Like I am a hard-core, out-of-control addict or something. I don't need to be taken care of River. I actually find that drives me crazy more than anything about you. Your need to 'rescue' me."

"Okay, I can appreciate that. And I can't lie – it's true that I want to help you out in any way possible. But is that a crime? Isn't that what I'm *supposed* to do?"

"I don't know. Is there a rulebook? Is there a certain way I am *supposed* to respond to your offer? I need to think on it for a while. Is that alright with you?"

"Sure, take all the time you need. And any time you want to talk — "

"Yeah, yeah."

Knowing Sylvia and her moods, I have learned when to stop pushing. Her eyes are roaming around anyway and that is a cue that she is about to change the subject. I beat her to it.

"So, tell me more about this Jonah guy you run into at Lydie's house. He sounds like quite the character." I thought this was safe subject matter since Sylvia often cracks jokes at his expense.

"No, let's not go there. In fact, I have to get over to the bus loop very quickly because Mui is supposed to be cooking dinner for me tonight. It would be rude of me to be late."

"Are we okay?" I ask her in the raw and awkward moment that follows.

She bends over and gives me a hug. "You worry too much, River. What do I need a mother for when I have you?" She chides.

Her small show of affection is positive. I feel some measure of accomplishment. She is a delicate bird, this Sylvia. One has to have extreme patience and the most delicate kid gloves when dealing with her.

CHAPTER NINE
Lydie

In springtime in Vancouver, it looks like the place where fair-
ies live. I walk down a path on campus and little white petals
fall down all around me. Big fluffy blossoms almost knock
me in the head. Other pretty flowers like the rhododendrons
and the azaleas are all around here. Huge slimy slugs crawl
beside me and in front of me, but I don't step on them. Sylvia
never does either, but she says 'cause it's disgusting to see snail
guts on her shoes. I step around the slugs so they won't die.
They not pretty to look at but they have their place too in
this world. My daddy always taught me to respect every living thing, even the ones that end up grinded in our bellies
– *especially* those ones.

Got to get together with Sylvia tonight. Got my last term
paper due next week and have to get Sylvia to look it over.
She a good writer and she find things the spellcheck can't see.
Like *their* and *they're*. She always on me about using quotation

marks. I never do that because I don't believe it look right. I mean, you just know when someone's talking – you don't need no " " up in the air. Too fancy for me. I just like sticking to the bare bones in my papers. To heck with all the fancy squiggles. I'm too old to keep track of so many. One professor said I was being *subversive* – guess that's a good thing. I had to look it up in the dictionary, though. One of those big fancy words that I don't use to talk with. Writing things down is not the way it was always done. Used to be that the first peoples told all stories by mouth, not by writing. Up until my time, all there was were the stories told to us over centuries by the elders. Then when residential schools were dreamed up by the people in the churches and the white government, everything changed.

I sing a song to myself as I walk along my path to the Longhouse. Songs are like stories. Well really, they are stories. And everyone should have those. Longhouse that I go to isn't a real longhouse from the olden days, put up by Indian men. No sir, some white construction workers build it a few years ago and make it to look like the traditional houses that the old ones used to live in. The university design it for a place for Indians to hang out together. *First Nations Longhouse* the sign says outside. I sometimes call Sylvia a Second Nation and she laugh. She know what I mean.

Inside the Longhouse, I sit on a bench and take out my thermos with hot soup inside it. It was hot this morning. Now it's kinda cold. My good friend Lenora comes and sits beside me. What going on here today? I ask her. I see booths set up around the whole Great Room. Information Fair for Student Services, Lenora tell me.

We eat quietly on our sandwiches, watching all the stranger people who sit behind the tables, passing out flyers to a few Indian kids who walk from booth to booth. Lots of white people work for those student services. Used to be I was scared of white people, after the Choutla School, where there was some real bad white people. Can't trust them, I thought. Further south I traveled, the more white people there was. But one thing I see was that the white children weren't no different than Indian kids. I babysat three little white kids up in Prince George. They called me grandma and loved to give hugs and kisses. Real sweet and lovable. I see them be scared when their daddy came home mad and swinging for a fight. I stopped being scared of white people at that time. Other things scared me more than a skin color. Like how could a daddy give his own daughter broken ribs?

Lenora and me are sitting close to one of the display tables. Two young pretty white girls sit there gossiping with each other more than talking to the lookers. Pretty girls' table has a sign saying they from UBC Sorority Society. They both have shiny yellow hair and one has hers done up in a hundred tiny little braids like a Jamaican. Only she lot whiter than a Jamaican person. The one with the head full of braids looks up all of a sudden and says, do you smell that? Someone's smoking dope!

Lenora and I look around and giggle. The white girl stands up and starts sniffing the air like a dog. I can smell weed, she says. Someone's smoking pot! Pretty girl says so loudly that people all around are looking at her. Lenora gets up slowly and walks over to the girl. Excuse me, Lenora says to the girl, that not dope you smell – that is sweet-grass burning. Sage and cedar and sweet-grass – someone is doing a smudge over there!

The girl look real embarrassed so Lenora pat her arm and tell her, it's okay, it does smell stinky if you never been around it before.

Lenora walk back to me and we both laughing with our eyes.

Later that day I am just off the bus and waddling down the street to my old rental house. I like my house even though it not a big fancy one like some of the ones in Vancouver. It was built in the 1920s, the landlord told me, so it old and rickety like me. It has a little attic with a window in the front and one in the back too. I like to go up there because when I look out the window in the front I see all the goings-on down in the street. And when I go to sit by the window in the back of the attic I see the mountains to the north. It make me smile just to think of those big snow-covered mountains, blue and purple in the distance. They are the direction of home for me.

My smile falls down my face when I come around the corner and see Jonah on the front porch, half lying down, shirt untucked and messy, with a case of beer beside him.

Get up, you fool, I tell him. He grovel around mumbling and not making sense. He trying to eat cold pizza out of a box I threw out in the alley trash two days ago. But it's hard as rock and he can't chew it with his jelly jaws full of the alcohol.

What you doing out here in the cold rain? I ask him. He tell me he hanging out, getting closer to nature. I tell him it look more like he getting closer to death. He laugh, or try to, and snorts and coughs up phlegm. But it not funny. I see that he is still wearing his blue uniform shirt from work at the mechanic shop. His little embroidered name below the collar is so neat and cute in the pretty slanted writing: *Jonah*. I still see my little boy before me: his tears, his smiles, his softness. Jonah light another cigarette. I reach down and take that cigarette right out of his hand. He so drunk that he no match for a quick old woman like myself. I throw the butt down on the sidewalk and go chasing after it to squish it with my rubber boot. Jonah jerks up and stands wobbly, then down the wooden steps and across the wet grass. He has no shoes. He slips down at the edge of the road and lands on his belly. My boy, my boy. I go to him and help him up. Grass stains all over his nice work shirt. He leans on me and staggers. I pull him back over the lawn, up the stairs and through the house to his bedroom in the back. He fall down onto the bed and I sit next to him, stroking his hair, just thinking how lucky I am to have him here with me and not gone away to prison like Mitchell or in some gutter all by his lonesome self. I can remember when he was a young boy, just a baby still. All babies start out the same – so much pure love and fun and happiness. Sometimes I wish we could be babies forever.

Next day Jonah gets up and showers before coming over to hug me in my chair. He thanks me for washing up his work shirt. He say he sorry about the day before and he promise me he cook me some bacon and eggs.

CHAPTER TEN
Sylvia

Medicine Hat is where I lost my virginity at the Cowboy Motel on the south side of the Trans-Canada Highway – to some carnival guy passing through town. I was sixteen and in love. He was much older and gone two days later. Good thing I had a condom with me from sex-ed class in high school. When River asked who "took" my virginity, I said no one *took* it, I offered it up to a traveling businessman. River didn't need to know about the Cowboy Motel. There is a lot from my past that River doesn't know about. I really don't think he would like me if he knew some of the sleazy stuff I have done. And now he wants to live with me. My intuition is telling me that would be a very bad idea. That somehow, living with River would perpetually trap me in a destructive, self-loathing, defensive posture. Maybe I *am* being too sensitive. But isn't the person you love supposed to bring out the best in you, rather than the worst? Or at least, the honest, genuine person that you are?

Hopping off the bus today for some study time at Lydie's before one of our final exams. I take my disabled bicycle from the bike rack on the front of the bus and push it up the road to Lydie's house. My packsack is heavy with books, and I try to balance it on the bike seat so I will not have to bear the full weight of it. It thuds to the porch floor when Lydie lifts it off the bike seat at her house.

"No wonder you skinny girl!" She laughs. "This pack weighs more than you do!"

"Is Jonah home?" I ask, eager to get him working on my bike. Lydie said he could fix it and volunteered his free labor.

"Jonah be home in a little bit. He'll fix your bike up all better, don't you worry."

"You sure he doesn't mind you volunteering him to do this?"

"Nope. He owes me many favors. Plus I think he likes you."

"What? Why would you think that?"

"Oh, I don't know. He ask a lot of questions about you. But if he heard me telling you this he would say mind your own business you gossipy old lady! Come, we have tea."

We settle onto the couch in the dark little living room and drink the thick tea that Lydie made. She has a paper she wants me to look over first before we study. But I hear the rumble of a bike outside. And feel my heart jump up a few notches. Seconds later Jonah bangs the door open and says, "Hey buddy, I got some fresh cash for you." He produces a wad of Canadian Tire money and stuffs it into a jar on the fridge. Lydie's face lights up like a child receiving a gift from Santa.

"Oh, hi there, Sylvia." Jonah nods as he notices me sitting beside his mother.

"Only store in the world that produces its own currency." I smirk at him.

"Well, Ma's rich by Canadian Tire standards anyways," Jonah says, nodding toward the overflowing pickle jar.

"He just jealous 'cause I almost got enough points for a bread-making machine." Lydie retorts with a big yellow-toothed smile on her face. It's funny to see these two bicker.

I watch as Jonah fills his mother's fridge with eggs, milk, and bread that he must have juggled on his street bike. A couple of six-packs of beer hitched a ride with him too. But he seems more sober than when I saw him last. Lydie chatters on about what other prizes she has procured with her points.

"Jonah, I brought my bike over so you could have a look at it – Lydie said you would – it hasn't been working for like, eight months now. Gears or something."

"Sure. Was that it outside the door?" He's already moving out the screen door and lifting the bike up and into the house. He hoists it effortlessly onto the kitchen table and begins twirling the pedal around, looking closely at the mechanics of the thing. He leaves briefly without saying anything and returns with a kit of small tools. I go back to sit with Lydie and continue to glance through the paper she wanted me to edit. But I am distracted by Jonah's quiet presence, as he works diligently on my broken bike.

After a half hour, he calls me over.

"Sylvia, see here, this is what the problem was. Hard to diagnose but an easy fix, really." He begins explaining to me exactly what the trivial problem was, but I am not at all into the technical description. Instead, I watch him speak. His jaw is large and powerful (I can see the muscles of his temple tighten and relax as he talks), his face is smooth but with hard lines and edges. Jonah's eyes are dark and deep-set; they appear at one moment alert, then, a split second later, weary. I always get the sense from watching his face that he looked like a grown man long before he was even technically an adult. In fact, I cannot even imagine him as a boy; he appears so much a mature man. But he is not that much older than me. Maybe thirteen years or so.

"Thank you, Jonah. For fixing it. The thing has been leaning against the side of my apartment for months because I have been too unmotivated and too penniless to take it to a shop."

"You have a boyfriend. Couldn't he have fixed it?"

"River? Uh, no. He's just not handy that way. He's musical and artistic but not knowledgeable about the mechanics of how things work. More of an intellectual," I explain self-consciously.

"That's too bad," Jonah replies, but not in a mean manner, not joking. More like he seriously regrets that I am saddled with such useless baggage. In fact, I feel his sincerity so strongly that I abandon the practised defence of River that I usually fall back on when I'm in Jonah's presence.

"Okay Sylvia, you can bike to California on this gal – she's good for another thousand miles," Jonah says as he lifts the bike up and off the table as though it was weightless. I follow him out to the porch where he sets it down; his arms flexed and so taut I can see the movement of his muscles under his shirt. He has large, beautiful, capable arms.

"Time for study!" Lydie sings out to me.

We resume our quiet work in the living room for only another ten minutes before the phone rings. Lydie answers, happily launching into a conversation with Mitchell, who's calling from The Big House. Miffed but understanding that our study time has now been indefinitely delayed, I wander over to the kitchen to help Jonah break some eggs in a frying pan.

"I didn't know you could cook," he says with a straight face.

"I can't. I just like to take my aggression out on inanimate objects that crack under very little pressure."

"They're actually alive, you know."

"What – eggs? No they're not!"

"Yes, they're aborted baby chickens."

"Well they are dead by the time they make it to the supermarket shelf."

"How do you know?" He looks at me sideways with a smirk.

Good question, I think to myself. *I don't really know what the hell an egg is anymore than I know what an oyster is. Do those things have brains?* "If you are so pro-life, then why are you eating these poor dead baby chickens?" I ask him.

"I didn't say I was pro-life. Just giving you something to think about, is all."

Jonah takes off his leather vest and rolls up the sleeves of his shirt. He sees me eyeing up the plethora of tattoos on his arms —some rough and amateurish, others artistic and clearly works of professional pride.

"Impressed?" he says chuckling. I must have looked for too long.

"You certainly have a lot of ink on you. Do they go all the way up your arm?"

"Yeah. This side is the bad part of me — " he indicates his left arm, "and this side is the good part of me." He runs his hand gently along the images on his right arm. The left arm shows dark scenes of gravestones with assorted names on them, prison bars, Grim Reaper-type characters and demons. The right side had a likeness of the Virgin Mary, a fist of strength, feathers, a powerful stylized eagle, and a little girl.

"Who's this?" I ask, touching the image of the small female child who is kneeling and praying, her head bowed.

"That's my daughter," Jonah says. He had never said anything about her to me before. But I don't have the guts to pry about this one. I hardly know the guy.

I realize I have kept my finger on his skin just a little too long.

"Do the two sides of artwork come together on your back or something?" I ask as he returns to the spitting eggs on the stove.

"No. The story isn't finished yet." His eyes pass over the toaster and the tomatoes he had lined up on the counter.

"Sylvia! Come on, girl – we need to get back to work! Come read my paper!" Lydie calls from the next room.

"I know, but you were on the phone."

"It was my Mitchell calling from the Correctional Institute. I had to talk to him – there's only certain times when he's allowed to call."

"Correctional Institute" is what Lydie calls the place where her other son is incarcerated. She has never said "prison" as long as I've known her. Sometimes I think she fancies that he is away at a boarding school or something, but then I recognize that judgemental, paternalistic thing that creeps into my thoughts a lot when I'm with Lydie. Why is that? River would be analysing it into a paper on race relations if he were able to hear my thoughts.

"Go on then." Jonah nudges me out of his way.

"Wait, whose names are on all the gravestones?" I ask pointing to his left arm.

"Those are friends of mine that I lost. Killed, or killed themselves. Overdose and that sort of thing. One was stabbed while we were in a gang fight in prison."

"You were in prison too?"

"Yeah. But no more questions for now. You go study. Help my mom get good grades. Keeps her mind off her bad boys."

The following day I am at my Auntie Chris' pad watching a hockey game with her. Even though we are inland transplants, we are both die-hard Vancouver Canuck fans. Her pouffy hair is scrunched back into a tight little ball, but frizzy pieces can't resist popping out and defying gravity. She complains about her unruly 'do but it gives her that certain mysterious vampy aura that the men just love – that and the fact that she is amply endowed in the bosom area, and is single and childless in her late thirties. At a commercial break, Auntie Chris asks (after three big jaw-extending yawns from me), "Where's River tonight?"

"Oh, I don't know…some save-the-Spotted-Owl-from-the-loggers rally on campus." I yawn again, falling deeper into her plush white chesterfield. I could swim in this thing.

It's really comfortable in here. Much more so than the outside world. I would have continued living with my aunt longer if it hadn't been for her annoying little habit of bringing home guys from work. The walls in her apartment are thin and she is a rather vocal person, so it was a tad uncomfortable for my sister and me. We would drop hints here and there and mention that she sure had a lot of "friends" from work, but she would just laugh it off. At first I thought she was serial dating every single one of her male co-workers, but she works as a bank teller, so how many men could possibly be employed there? Who knows where she finds them.

"How come you aren't with River at the rally?" Auntie Chris asks as she pulls off the rubber band and allows the mass of blonde fuzz to fully inflate and spill down to her shoulders.

"I kind of got worn out on the whole thing, I guess. Not the cause – the people. Bunch of rich kids who grew their hair long and didn't wash it for two years. Tying themselves to giant cedar trees. Meanwhile their daddies and mommies are doctors and lawyers and corporate CEOs. Seems a little hypocritical somehow. But someone has to do it – protest stuff – I guess it's good that they do. But to me, hanging out with them after a while felt like hanging out with kids who were going through a phase – you know, like it's hip that they all look and talk and think alike."

"Thought you were into that kind of stuff. Like your dad – he was really into rocks and trees and all that natural stuff."

"My real dad?"

"Yeah. Pierre. He was kind of a dick – kept to himself,

did his work for the department of natural resources, but a smart guy from what I remember. Broody, quiet, introverted guy. You never knew that about him?"

"I don't know a whole lot about him, really. Just that he's an 'asshole.' My mom took up with Floyd when I was only four and she never much talked about my real dad after that. I wonder about him though – Pierre."

"Floyd's a dick too, but your real dad at least had some brains. I knew him when your mom first met him. Pierre was just too much of an intense person – the French in him maybe. Just up and left your mom and went off to Northern Quebec. Had his own demons, I suppose. She was so pissed – rightfully so – she never wanted to have anything to do with him again. He used to write sometimes, you know, to you and your sister. But your mom never let you see the letters. They were all in French anyways, which she couldn't understand a word of and that pissed her off even more. He did it on purpose, she thought. But his English was never that good. So she just tore them up."

"I never knew that he was trying to reach out to us. My mom never said anything about it. I always was curious about my real dad – like what does he look like, does he have any hideous genetic diseases – but never really gave much thought to him being a 'real' person. He was always this ghost figure in our family past. You'd hear an allusion to him once in a while but that was it. It was never a friendly allusion either. Might be neat to look him up sometime, though. Gosh, it's scary just saying that out loud."

"You know Sylvia, just thinking, I heard about a year ago that Pierre was working over there in Abbotsford, doing some soil studies or something. You should see about contacting him if you want to find out more about the other half of your heritage. The French part of you. Your mom doesn't have to know."

"Yeah best if we kept that one under wraps because she has already started the documentation to have me disowned. Wouldn't want to aggravate it any more."

"Oh it's not that bad with her is it? Yeah? I mean, your mom's a bitch for treating you that way. I love her as my sister and I feel sorry for her for losing a son, but I hate the way she's taking all that shit about Tommy out on you two girls. You especially. You handle it so well. It would've made me a basketcase."

"That's what many years of intensive therapy and a little self-mutilation will do for you. I'm kidding about the self-mutilation. But don't get me wrong – I will have mother-issues until the day I die. You know, all that 'Electra Complex' crap."

"Well, I'm not pushing you, but maybe talking to your real dad will help out the situation a little bit – by answering some questions. I know you must have issues with him abandoning you guys, but maybe you can learn more about yourself if you meet him. He's so close, being in Abbotsford… I'm not pushing you. Just putting it out there into the universe." Auntie Chris's voice trails off as she ruffles her hair with her hands.

"Huh. I'll ponder it for a bit. I might just do that."

The hockey game heats up and we don't linger on the father issue. Though I do wonder what it would be like to meet him. What would I say? *Hi Dad, I'm the one you left behind remember? Me and my sis. And oh yeah, I'm the one you read about in those news reports – you know, the one who left her baby brother outside and he went missing.'* I wonder what he'd say.

CHAPTER ELEVEN
Lydie

Sexual Textual Politics – now there's a title! I use this book for writing my final essay for Feminist Literary Theory class. Sylvia was going through the French Feminist Theory part of the book with me – weird stuff. Those French girls must have some incest going on in their olden days or something. They a little obsessed with all the Phallus stuff. Big fancy name for dick. Why not just call it dick? With a little d? Makes it seem like what it really is – just a flap of stinky skin that hang there and the dumbo attached to it always wants to play with it.

Rooney was one of those dumbos – thought his dick was some big deal. Thought he was some big deal – always had to be the boss of me. Lucky for me, Old Man die when I was still young. Otherwise I would'a been a bitter old lady. But nope, buried Old Man and his dick in the cemetery outside Teslin and never had to hear from him again. Or his dick. And I sure don't miss it.

Life there in Teslin wasn't all that bad. I should tell you about the good times when I was young. I live with my mum and dad and baby sister – three years younger than me. She dead now too but she was my baby sister back then. We play with apple dolls my mum made from peeled apples stuck on a stick with scraps of linen and rags for dresses. The apple was the doll's head and we decorated with buttons for eyes and nose and mouth. Mum put rabbit fuzz on their heads so they had white hair too – like an old lady. Thing about those apple dolls is that they were alive! They start out white, shiny and wet like a newborn baby then they get brown color, then they start to dry out and get all wrinkly. Pretty soon they wither up like an old lady (like the way I look now) and after a couple years they start to rot like a dead person. They live a whole life, just like a human person. Anyway, me and my sister play with those homemade toys and help Mum with laundry and sewing she took in at the cabin in Teslin. She work for only a little money, cleaning clothes and making moccasins but those days it bought supplies like lard and flour and once in a while a new pair of mukluks – those are boots you know. We only wore mukluks in wintertime or up on the mountains – with all the cold snow you had to. But in summertime our feet got hard as rawhide from running and horsing around with bare feet. They get real dirty in between the toes, I think I still have dirt from when I was a kid down in there. But the feet never get stinky in the summer 'cause they not shoved inside a sweaty, tight shoe. Also, sometimes when it was hot, we kids run around naked, jumping in and out of the rivers and lakes, rolling our bare bums in the weeds and pine needles. It felt so good, I always wanted to do it since then but they would probably lock me up in jail or a mental hospital thinking I was a crazy old Indian.

We moved around a lot back in those days. We moved with the seasons, with the animals, or because someone was sick or someone needed help. We moved from winter camps to summer camps and up the traplines and down the lakes and rivers. Seems like we were always traveling and it was a fun time for a youngster. We walked everywhere back then – no cars until the Alaska Highway came through in the Forties, but even then we weren't allowed in cars on the highway until after the war was over. The road from Carcross to Teslin was just a trail before the highway came. And we walked it many times. When my sister and I were kids, our muscles were strong and thin because we do so much work and walk so many miles. All the kids were like that back then, even the sick ones. Kids today are so lazy – so fat with sugar puffs and no exercise. Now kids can ride on a bus or watch television all day – they don't have to go out chasing rabbits like we used to. Many things change in my lifetime, maybe the most change in centuries.

Old people in the families told stories all the time. Seems like that was the most important thing for them to do. And we young people was supposed to be learning from them. All the stories told so many times I have them living in my head, even though they are very old and have been around for a thousand years. The old people use stories to teach the younger ones. They tell stories to teach what is good and bad, and to trick us into things too, like not to stay out past dark or the mosquito man would kidnap us away. The elders say it is important to tell those stories so the old ways aren't lost.

top. I try desperately to get some soap on the jacket out of the dispenser but it is bone dry. Then I just try scrubbing my coat with water and paper towels. It smells disgusting now. I scrub harder and harder to get the crud and stench off the coat. It is a coat that I had when I was eight or nine years old.

Just then, someone bursts through the swinging door.

"Sylvia – what the hell are you doing?!" the grown-up version of my sister screeches at me.

"Nothing." I feel small and guilty – the little kid version of me.

"Just leave the frigging thing behind and quit wasting your time with that," Jessie says as she grabs the coat and throws it on the floor. She takes me by the sleeve and pulls me out of the dirty restroom, leaving the coat, and the mess, behind.

Then I wake up.

Ring, ring. Come on you nerd! I'm cradling the phone to my ear with my shoulder while my hands work idly at the stitching on this green dress I have been trying to finish for months.

"Y'hello?" Her singing voice tinkles into the phone.

"Hey sister, how's it going?" I drop my sewing project for a minute – it's good to hear her voice. But I won't mention the dream to her. She doesn't need to know about that embarrassing subconscious stuff that oozes from my brain.

"Oh hi, Silly! What's up?" Jessie draws out the *ahhh* sound in the "what." She has called me Silly ever since she first started talking. She couldn't pronounce Sylvia correctly – but her inability to enunciate never slowed her mouth down.

"Just calling to see how the dead-body job thing is going lately." Jessie has been working as a "Skeletal Disarticulator" on a work-study grant for the last few months. She receives donated dead bodies – animal bodies – and dismembers them to get down to the bones, which she has to classify and label for study at the university biology and zoology departments.

"It's going good – I had an African boar to dissect the other day. Donated from the Toronto Zoo after he croaked of old age. I was having a bitch of a time getting the brain matter out of the thick skull so I brought it home to boil it overnight, since I couldn't just leave it boiling in the lab unattended."

"No, of course not. How the hell did you bring the pig head home with you?"

"Oh, I just wrapped it in some plastic bags with ice – so it wouldn't smell too bad – and shoved it in my duffle bag. It was really heavy and bulky and only one guy on the subway asked me what I was carrying."

I can envision Jessie on the Toronto subway with her snowboarder's tuque, oversized Jackie-O sunglasses, and her vintage 1980s duffle bag full of a decapitated pig's head – and her not thinking there was anything wrong with that whatsoever. "So what did you tell the guy?"

"The truth. He wanted to see it but I told him the smell would probably knock him unconscious. And when I got home I almost knocked Phil unconscious because I was in the shower when he came in and he went to the stove to see what I was cooking for dinner – it was giving off a wonderful Easter-dinner aroma. He started stirring the pot and this big warthog head was staring up at him – I hadn't extracted the eyeballs yet. He was really upset about that. Whoops!"

"I could see why that would be a little perturbing. Anyway, speaking of upsetting anomalies, I heard a little something about our bio-dad the other day."

"Deadbeat dad? That Pierre guy?"

"Yes, it seems our biological is now living and working in Abbotsford out here in British Columbia – at least that's what Auntie Chris heard."

"Yeah I know, she told me a little while ago. She didn't know if she would tell you and she swore me to secrecy because she was afraid it would freak you out too much. Did it?"

"You knew? Why didn't you tell me?"

"Because I didn't want to set you back four years in your therapy sessions."

"Thanks, sis. How thoughtful of you and Auntie. I feel so protected." Dropping the sarcasm, I ask, "Didn't you get the slightest bit curious about contacting Pierre?"

"Naw, that stuff is ancient history. I don't really give a care either way. Let bygones be goons. That's my enlightened philosophy."

"Huh. I was thinking about contacting him. What do you think?"

"Well, if it's something you feel is really necessary for your mental well-being, then go for it. You have my support. I don't want to talk to the guy. I wouldn't mention it to Mom though – that would really knock her off the bridge into Lake Hysterical."

"No kidding. Have you heard from her lately?"

"About a month ago I called her. She was her usual joyous

self. I could hear her wheezing and chain-smoking on the other end of the line. She just bitched and complained about Floyd and what a lazy ass he is. Still not working you know – he continues to claim disability because of the back injury thing but he's always off helping his brother do body work on rusty old beaters."

"At least he has a steady income flowing in once a month – the disability check."

"Yeah, you could call it that, I guess. Thank goodness they can live rent-free in Grampa's old house – otherwise they'd be in some tough financial shape. But now that Boxcar Huey has bit the biscuit, Mom doesn't have a drinking buddy anymore to mooch her liquor from."

Jessie is referring to the old man who lived at our house for most of our teenage years. His real name was Huey Bonnie Johnson. He was known as Boxcar Huey around Medicine Hat because he reportedly "rode the rails" during the Great Depression. He was an old homeless drunk that my mom brought home one day in the 1980s, saying he was a distant cousin of hers – two or three times removed – and she gave him Tommy's old room to stay in.

"Gosh I wonder if the stink has aired out of Boxcar Huey's room yet?" I quip. The guy never bathed when he was alive. Never. And he used a handheld plastic urinal in his bedroom. You can imagine the smell that crept out from under the door, which he always kept closed. My sister and I used to hold our noses and dare each other to run past his door yelling, "Take a bath Boxcar Huey! You smell like stinky, rotten poo-ey!" It was really funny at the time.

"I imagine Mom has cleaned out the room by now.

Remember how long it took her to clean it out after Tommy? Months and months."

"Yeah. Is Mom still working at the corner store?"

"Every weekend. That's how she keeps up with The Hat gossip, don't you know. Her and Aunt Ginny sitting there smoking, trashing all the young gals who had babies in high school coming in to get milk and bread and cigarettes."

"Like they should talk – those two both had kids and never even finished high school, never really left The Hat."

"Oh well, whatever keeps them ticking. You should call Mom sometime. You know she'd probably never call you. It would be way beyond her sphere of comfort."

"And why would I want to stir up that pot?" I pick up my sewing again and work the needle in through the tough fabric and out again.

"Well, why then do you want to contact the sperm donor?"

"Good question. I just…I…I don't really know. Just to see if there's any of us in him. Auntie Chris said he was brainy."

"Yeah but obviously had no guts – I mean the guy couldn't handle being saddled with a wife and two kids so he split to go work with rocks in the bush of Quebec – what a winner."

"I wonder if he even speaks enough English to hold a conversation with me. My French is really rusted-out."

"Well you'll probably get more out of him than you would out of Mom."

"That is true. Are you still able to get the time off to come to my graduation?"

"Yes indeed. Phil can't come though because he has a tri-athlon event up at Blue Mountain. I was supposed to be in it too, but it's no big deal. There's another one in the summer we'll be doing."

"You two are so sporty. River is always trying to get me out hiking but I never have enough time or energy for that stuff. And my bike just got fixed after months of lying around broken."

"Too many potato chips for you and not enough time in the gym. Pretty soon you'll have those rubber things of fat flopping from your underarms like Mom does. How is River doing anyway? You guys ever planning on moving in together? After graduation would be the perfect time – it will be like forward momentum in your life."

"What is it with moving in with River? He recently started to bug me about it too. Are you guys in on this together? I'm thinking that it's not going to happen. In fact, I don't even know if I'm going to stay in Vancouver." *I can't believe I just said that – where the hell did that come from?*

"Really? Leave Vancouver? I thought you loved it out there?"

"I do, I do. But maybe it's time for a change. I got the itch lately."

"Where would you go? You've practically sworn off ever returning to Alberta."

"I don't know, Jessie. I really have no idea. Probably some-where smaller than here. A different pace of life. The Yukon maybe." *I can't believe that I said that out loud.*

"Wow! That's outta a goat's ass! The Yukon is in a different category altogether. Where did that come from? Did your elder friend Lydie talk you into that?"

"No. Well, yes, she tells me lots about the Yukon, but it's

something I've been kicking around for a little while. I just feel restless here in the big city lately. Got the inclination to move somewhere smaller, but where none of the locals knew me growing up. Cozy but still anonymous. Do you understand what I'm talking about?"

"Not really. Maybe it's because you are so close to graduating and all the stress from exams is exacerbating your anxiety."

"Perhaps you're right. But I had this weird conversation with Lydie's son Jonah and now I can't get the idea out of my head – leaving here – that is. It's really bugging me – what he said."

"You never mentioned that Lydie had a son. Is he single, cute? Wait – he must be a lot older than you if his mom is in her eighties."

"Yeah, he's quite a bit older than me, but Lydie had him when she was in her forties so I think he's only around late thirties or so."

"That is ancient, sis. I thought you were into younger guys like River – what is he, two years younger than you?"

"Yes. But you're taking it the wrong way. It's not like I'm into Jonah, romantically speaking. He's an interesting guy and he's just being friendly to me, that's all. I bet Lydie told him about the Tommy kidnapping thing and so now Jonah feels sorry for me. He wants to be my bud or something."

"Why did you tell Lydie about what happened to Tommy?"

"I just thought she should know, is all. I'm pro-honesty and openness. Transparency, and all that stuff."

"I never talk about that stuff. Makes me too depressed."

"And playing with dead bodies all day doesn't make you depressed?"

"No, that's different. When I graduate – in like, ten years – and become a pathologist, then I'll be helping people by figuring out how their loved ones died. Making a difference – giving closure to families."

"Well I hope you are a better pathologist than the hand-ies who worked on Tommy's bones. No closure there for our family."

"That's what motivates me every day. Tommy. But I don't dwell on it in a negative way – I just think of it as a type of magic to be able to work with remains and figure things out from there. Like a jigsaw puzzle, putting together the pieces and making sense of something tragic for the ones left behind."

Mui comes up beside me on the sofa and gestures wildly with her hands and her eyes – something about a miscommunication with her girlfriend and she desperately needs to use the phone.

"Jess, I'm going to have to call you back later. Mui needs to use the phone or else she's going to have a hernia or something."

"Yeah, later. Take care."

Mui grabs the phone from my hand the second after it hits the cradle and runs wildly into her room. She begins sobbing into the phone incoherently. I hate when she has her little breakdowns – she is so vocal about them. Way too much estrogen and emotion for me to deal with. I can see I'm not going to get much more done on this dress today so I set it down in the basket with all my other half-finished sewing projects. I grab my sweater and head out the door for a walk.

It's raining on Broadway Avenue. Of course. I have to walk on my tiptoes and heels to avoid the worms. But the air feels extremely refreshing after the overheated, stuffy basement apartment. I realize I have been sweating. Profusely. *Huh. Psychosomatic.* The content of the conversation with my sister has affected me more intensely than I thought it would. And the sight of these worms is not easing my angst. I just need to sit here on this bench and think for a bit...put my feet up so that the worms and slugs will be at bay.

Maybe I should talk to Lydie about this. The B-Line bus is pulling up right now. I don't have my bus pass but I have some change in my sweater pocket. Lydie will lend me some coinage to get back home. I hop on the bus and forty minutes later I am walking up Lydie's front path. The inner door is ajar and the screen door is unlatched so I knock three times and let myself in.

"Lydie? You home?"

I can hear some movement in the back of the house, then a minute later Jonah wanders out wearing only a pair of jeans, his feet and chest bare and shining with sweat.

"What are you doing here?" he asks, not making eye contact.

"I just came by to talk to Lydie. I wanted to get her advice on something."

"She's not here. She had an exam on campus this afternoon."

"Oh darn, that's right. I knew about that. I forgot – so wrapped up in my own — " My explanation is cut short by the sight of a half-dressed vixen sleepily sauntering out from Jonah's room.

"What's up Jo? Who's this?" She has a husky voice, and casually slips a tank top over her black lace bra. My face is surging red.

"Sorry for…interrupting…or showing up unannounced. I'll leave." I feel like a child standing here awkwardly in my homemade Daffy Duck sweater and the worn old tennis shoes I had thrown on earlier, never thinking I would venture far from home.

"No worries hun, I was just going. He's all yours." The woman laughs loudly. She is a good ten years older than me and although her clothes look slutty, she is very attractive. Long, dark hair and pale skin, stunning bone structure. She lights up a cigarette, takes a long drag, exhales, then kisses Jonah passionately, groping his ass with her free hand. Jonah acts as though she has some sexual, magnetic pull on him, and I can see why.

"I'll see you later, sweetie," she says flippantly. She grabs her large leather purse from the kitchen table – it has a racoon tail swinging off it – and slips out the door, leaving a cloud of smoke and perfume in her wake.

"So…" Jonah says, looking down at the floor.

"Who was that? Your girlfriend?"

"No. No girlfriend. Just a friend. We meet up at the bars every so often. Seems like we always end up…"

"In bed together? Like a fuck friend?" I say, regaining my gall and my pride.

"You're too young to be talking like that," Jonah says. He fiddles with dishes in the sink, still not looking at me.

"Sure Jonah, I'm just a pre-teen right? What do I know about casual fucks?"

He finally turns his head to me slowly and looks me squarely in the face.

"Is it against the law? And how does my personal business concern you anyhow?"

I am momentarily speechless by his slow, deliberate words and steady gaze.

"I just thought you were...were...I should go," I mumbled as I hurried toward the door.

"Thought I was what?" Jonah called out.

Ignoring him, I escape down the stairs and the path to the street. He doesn't come after me. I can hear my heart pound in my head. *Low-life asshole,* I think, berating myself for ever entertaining any sentimental feelings toward Jonah.

On the very long walk home – I had not a cent to my name for bus fare – I decide that I must contact my real father. *I must.* Because it's killing me not knowing who he really is.

CHAPTER THIRTEEN
Lydie

This is the way to my last exam. This is the path I take. I looked it up on the campus map. I am singing *Whistle While You Work* – I love that kiddie song. Who sang that? The Seven Dwarfs? Makes me want to work harder. Best place to be in your brain when you're walking into a final exam. I'm a good student here these last five years. I was good student too when I went to the school at Carcross, got good marks I mean. Didn't always behave good, but most the time the school workers never knew. We Indian kids were good at hiding things.

They came for the second batch of Indian kids when I was twelve, year 1926. They took me and my sister and all the younger kids away on a horse wagon, just like the first time. Since I was older, I remember it perfectly. My mum had heard that they was coming – and knew she and Dad was too sickly to fight it this time, so she packed us a little bag with some clothes, a blanket, dried meat and berries, and an apple doll for each of us. She didn't know that the bag of home stuff was the first thing the school workers took away from us, I never saw it again but I never told my mum that. Anyway, I knew what was happening when they came to get us because I was older and I probably remember it better than all the younger kids. The parents all hugged their kids and some cried as the school workers rounded us up and herded us into the back of the wagon. It was like we were pigs going off to wherever it is they take pigs. My sister and some other little ones clung close to me. Some boys yelled and kicked and tried to jump off the wagon. But the school workers rode alongside with whips if anyone did get out. And they sure were good with those whips! The wagon pulled away from the village of Teslin with all the kids while the mummies and daddies watched. It broke their hearts inside them. Can you imagine seeing your children being taken away in a cart?

On the way to Carcross it was really hot and we had no water. It was late summer and the sun was beating down hard, making us sweat and want to stay very still. I tried to tell some stories to the younger kids to keep their minds busy, but they were too scared and too hot. On the road, on the way there, that we had walked many times, everything looked different. Maybe it was because we were riding on a wagon, rather than walking or maybe because it was our first time on that road without our parents. Either way, all the sights, the trees, the little lakes we passed seemed different. It was a different time, all of a sudden.

When we got there, to the school at Carcross, the wagon pulled past an English sign that none of us could read but

now I know it said *Choutla School*. We pulled up alongside a
big building that looked like a fancy barn with windows all
around it. I never seen a building that big before then. The
school workers and clergy greeted us with hellos and some
prayers and some seemed happy to see us but others were
shaking their heads. They separated the girls from the boys
right off the wagon and took us to separate rooms inside.
Right away the lady teachers told us to take off our home
clothes, get right naked, and gave us new uniforms to wear.
They burned our home clothes made of beaver cloth, moose-
hoof and button blanket because they said those clothes were
barbaric. The uniforms we had to wear were white ruffled
blouses, long dresses with a bib in front, and long underwears
– *and* black stockings we had to wear over the long underwears! Since it was summer, the ladies said we didn't have to
wear the long underwear, but even without them, the black
stockings were itchy wool that tickled our skin and made us
sweat all the time. Later, when the lady teachers weren't looking, some of the girls my age who had been there a while
showed me how to cut the stockings above the ankle so it
looked like I was wearing them all the way up my leg, but
the long dresses hid my bare legs underneath. It was cooler
that way, and when winter came, we always got new ones
anyway.

Next thing those fussy schoolteachers and clergy were
worried about was our hair. We noticed later at dinner that
all the boys had their hair taken right off! Shaved down bald
like a skinned hare – they looked so funny all of a sudden. Us
girls were allowed to keep our hair halfway long, above our
collars, but the dorm matrons had us wash each other's hair

really hard and taught us how to tie it up on our heads so that it didn't touch our dresses. I don't know why that was so important, but that was the rule – the hair couldn't fall down and touch our collars. Such silly little things you could get in big trouble for.

After they got us looking like they wanted us to look – they told us that we weren't allowed to speak our own languages anymore. Since me and the new kids couldn't speak English the way the older kids could, we had to keep quiet most of the time. That was the only way to stop getting a beating from one of the nasty school officials. They liked to hit us on the knuckles with a wooden stick if they heard us speak even one word of our home languages. And I got the feeling they really did like to hit little kids. Because they did it so much and for so little reason.

In the weeks that came next, the teachers tried to make sure we all caught up on learning English because it was in every song we sang, every school lesson and every prayer they taught us. A lot of the stuff they was teaching us was for the British Empire and the Church of England they told us – for the good of the civilization of the British Empire and to save our Christian souls. For a long time I never understood what the British Empire was. I thought it was a big angry man who lived across the lake from Carcross and he wanted everything to be his way, and wanted us Indian kids to turn into white people by eating porridge, porridge, porridge every single day. And I never understood what it meant to be a *Christian* soul – how was that different from a Tlingit or Tagish one?

And those teachers, not only had something against us kids, but our parents and grandparents too! They always tell us, again and again, not to listen to what our parents or grandparents say when we go home on short vacations. The teachers make real scary faces and say that the parents and all the old ones are *PAGANS* and we could end up like that too if we listened to what they had to say. We were so scared, none of us wanted to turn into *PAGANS* so we nodded our heads yes to the teachers that we would be careful not to let ourselves be turned into the *P* word.

Another thing the school officials did was give us English names because they said they was easier to pronounce. Since I already had an English name my mum gave as part of my full name, they just called me Lydie. I don't know if the teachers ever knew I was part white – if they did, they never showed it in any way. They treated me like all the rest. Except for Father MacAvoy. He liked to hear me read. He was a nice white person but really different from me. He was sad all of the time. All the other white people there seemed like they was mad all the time.

The teachers always made us sing songs. And not the songs that belonged to us – no way were we allowed to sing those songs! If we did sing Indian songs, then we got twenty lashings on the bare bottom by the headmaster – he was a mean, mean man. Some of the boys even got burned on their tongues I heard. The teachers taught us all new songs and told us to forget about any songs we learned at home because those old ones were *heathen* songs. The kind of songs they made us sing were Christian religious songs, based on Bible stories. Some of them were really creepy, also meant to scare little children, I guess. One song that was really upsetting to me was the *Coventry Carol*. It was based on the Bible story of the Massacre of the Innocents. That story tells about King Herod who ordered the killing of all male children who were two years old and under. The teachers used to say to us, "Imagine how terrible it would be to have your innocent young children killed because of a King who wanted to stay in power." And they would recite this prophecy from Jeremiah in the Old Testament to make sure we understood how terrible it was: "Thus says the Lord: A voice is heard in Ramah, lamentation and bitter weeping. Rachel is weeping for her children." I still remember it exactly.

Since I was twelve years old when I first heard that, it made me think more than maybe the young ones did. It made me think of how our parents felt when we was taken away by the Department of Indian Affairs to go to residential school. I thought it was a clever thing to see that similarity to the story of the Massacre of the Innocents. So I put up my hand and told the teacher what I thought. He didn't like that one bit. He called it "blasphemy" and it got me thirty lashes on the bare bum in front of the whole class. Then he made me stay after class was over and write down the words to the *Coventry Carol*, all the words, thirty times on the black board. Over and over again. My hands were aching and blistered by the time I finished.

CHAPTER FOURTEEN
Mitchell

The son-of-a-bitchin' guard rattles his baton across the bars of my cell. Just another day at Matsqui Correctional Institute.

"Wake up, Injun! Time for your head-doctor session."

"Huh?" I was too into the book I was reading.

"Therapy. Time to see the shrink."

I heave myself off the thin mattress pad and shuffle over to the door, back to the guard, hands into the pass-through so he can cuff me. No sense resisting this. Never does any good. Routine now, after six years.

Down the cellblock and into the long corridor where the shrink has his office.

"No, not him this time. They got you a new one. A young gal – new in town. You treat her good ya' hear? Or I kick your ass back to the reserve," the guard says. I wonder what he is talking about but follow him further down the hall into a room I have never been in before. There is a young woman sitting in a chair in the middle of the room. Pretty, well-dressed, but really young. She can't be more than thirty. She gestures for me to sit in the other chair directly across from her. The guard cuffs my hands to either side of the chair and gives me one further warning about how he'll cause me pain if I try anything with the new gal. And he goes to wait outside the closed door where he will periodically peer through the window at my back.

"What happened to Minsky?"

"Doctor Raminsky do you mean? He is still here. We just decided to try you out with a different therapist to see if that helps you any."

"You a therapist? You look too young to be doing that stuff."

"I assure you, I have all the proper training and certifications. Do you miss Doctor Raminsky? He would be interested to hear that you are noting his absence, seeing as how you never spoke a word to him in twenty sessions."

So she knows about that. My face feels hot all of a sudden. I wonder what else she knows about me.

"Tell me, Mitchell, your silence all that time with Doctor Raminsky – what was that about? Can you elaborate on that?"

"What's your name?" I ask her.

"Oh, yes, you're right. I should have introduced myself." She is flustered now. "My name is Carina Janson."

"Not doctor?"

"No, not yet. But soon. You can refer to me as Mrs. Janson."

"You married?"

"I prefer to keep my personal life private, please."

"I prefer to call you Carina. You don't seem old enough to be a missus."

"Very well then, if it makes you comfortable, you may call me by my first name. But please keep the personal questions out of these sessions. Now, back to what I was asking you, do you feel more comfortable speaking with a female rather than a male therapist?"

It's her who gets to ask all the questions.

"Don't like being alone with a guy," I say.

"Really? You know you're not really alone with the therapist, Mitchell – the guard is always watching."

"So then I'm alone with two guys."

"Do you feel like you need protection in here – I mean in prison?"

"You're naive if you think prison guards actually protect the inmates." I wonder if she has any idea what really goes on out in the cellblocks.

"Do you feel like your life is at risk?" Carina asks me, concerned.

"No. If you mean looking out for my back – I been doing that since I got here – over five years ago. Nothing scares me anymore. I fought back and guys know what I'm in for so they leave me alone out of respect for that. But I don't have no friends here either. Can't ever trust nobody here. You remember that, being so young and all, and a girl, you *especially* can't trust no one."

"Are you saying that you can't be trusted also?"

"Yep. You catch on quick."

"Well thank you for the warning. Is it easier for you to

talk to a female? I think I've gotten more out of you than Doctor Raminsky ever did."

"Sure it's easier to talk to a pretty girl than some old white asshole." But that's as far as I go. I can't tell her about the way a fist gets stuck in my throat when I'm alone in the small room with Raminsky – with any guy. No words can come out, 'cause that fist is jammed in there so tight it hurts.

"Mitchell, I was reading through your file and it says you are in for a conviction of manslaughter. Is that right?"

"Yeah. Ten years. No parole after seven for me – no time off for good behavior, those early fist fights took care of that. But my mum don't know. She always thinks I'll get out early. She's old you know – eighty-two. She can't come in here – I wouldn't let her. I tell her I'm not allowed to have visitors. I don't want her to see me in this place. She wants to see me when I get out. Before she dies."

"Is that important to you as well?"

That lump of a fist is starting to form. I can't talk about Lydie. It's too raw to think about my mum.

"Mitchell? That's fine if you don't want to answer that. But stay with me here. What about *why* you are in here? Can you tell me more about that?"

"Because I killed a guy."

"Yes, I realize that. But the events that led up to that… your motivations…what led you to take another human being's life?"

"He wasn't human. He wasn't animal either. Animals are better than that. What he did…"

"What did he do?"

Shit. Walked right into that one. Maybe this young therapist is better at her job than I first gave her credit for.

"Mitchell, I understand that you were institutionalized at a reform school when you were quite young. How did that happen?"

"Don't know. Judge took one look at me and saw some punk-ass Indian kid who ran away from school and stole some cars, so he sent me to the lock-up for bad boys."

"Brannan Lake Industrial School?"

"That's right. On Vancouver Island."

"What did that experience mean to you?"

How the hell can I answer that? What's it mean to you when they throw you away when you are just a kid, away from your mother and siblings and family? With no contact for five years with the outside world.

"Mitchell, what was it like – that time you spent at the reform school?"

I would hate to see the look on this pretty girl's face if I told her what it was really like. How the kids were forced to be slaves, to do hard physical labor every single day that would make a grown man cry. How our hands bled from blisters and splinters at the gravel pits. And how we were made to fight each other. All the blood, suicides, and self-mutilation. Then there was the time when one of the staff hit a twelve-year-old kid so hard he fell on one of those old fashioned metal desks and split his head open and died. His parents were told it was an accident and for those of us who saw it, we were told to lie about it. To make sure we did, we were kept in isolation cells for two weeks with no clothes. And it was winter.

"It was okay." *It was hell on earth.*

"It is now known there was a prevalence of abuse – particularly sexual abuse – at the school by male staff members. Is that something that was occurring when you attended?"

Attended? Like it was a choice. She says it like I was going to a regular high school or something. Sure we had choices: for punishments, we could either choose to be beaten with a wooden club with spikes on our bare asses, or voluntarily punch a pole covered in rope in the cellar until our knuckles bled. Overall, being tied-up in the crapper as punishment for stealing bread wasn't exactly my idea of voluntary attendance.

"Lot of bad shit happened."

"Were you victimized Mitchell?"

She wants to know if some supervisor fucked me up the ass or made me suck on his stinking, slimy cock. Or made some of the older boys do it to me so the fucker could watch beside the bed and get his rocks off. Or made me do it to some young kid when I was older so I could get a day pass out of the hell-hole.

"No."

"Mitchell, I understand that the man who you killed was a former staff member at Brannan Lake Industrial School. Was there some reason from your history that would provoke you into doing that?"

"You got the file there. Sure it tells you all about it." Sure it tells about Glen Waverly, the fucking dick supervisor with the pussy name. The one I ran into at a convenience store in Prince George years later, when I was in my thirties. He didn't recognize me as a grown man, at first, but he must have recognized the look in my eyes, because his eyes got real big and he headed out the door real quick. And something in me just snapped, and I headed out right after him. To his parked car that he was just getting into. I grabbed his hand and slammed the car door shut on his fingers. The fucker screamed like a little girl and the sound of it just made me crazier. I pummelled him in the head until he was down on the asphalt and it kept going and going and going, just like when he used to pump into me up the ass. And I wondered if it would ever stop. But my hand and arm kept going and smashing his ugly wrinkled old head into the pavement until it felt squishy, like a smashed pumpkin.

"That's why you got off with a charge of manslaughter isn't it? Rather than first-degree murder? Isn't it?"

"Got off? Yeah I got off real easy, me."

"I apologize, it was a poor choice of words on my part. But wasn't that why the jury felt pity for you – because the man had abused you at reform school?"

I shook my head. Yeah, those jury members probably thought they were doing some real humanitarian thing, sending an Indian to jail for ten years.

"Mitchell, you seemed to get somewhat emotional when you mentioned your mother. What was that about?"

"You got a mother? Yeah? You close to her?"

"We have a cordial relationship. But nothing personal from me, remember?"

"I was told my mother didn't want me no more. After the social workers decided to take me out of Brannon Lake because I was getting too many broken bones, I said that I wanted to go home and they said my mum didn't want me no more and that she was a drunk anyways. Then I had to go to some foster homes. Thing about it was, it wasn't true – about my mum. They lied to me, just a kid, those social workers fed all these lies to me about my mother. And none of it was true. I found out later my mum had been writing letters to me for years and trying to get me back, but they just kept telling me to forget about her 'cause she was no good. 'Till one day she found me at a group home in Whitehorse. And she told me it was all lies made up to keep us apart. And I didn't know whether to believe her or not. Imagine not knowing if you could trust your own mother. How would that feel to you?"

After the fifty-minute mark, the guard knocks on the glass window.

"Alright chief. Time's up. Session's over. Back to your house."

"Thank you for speaking with me Mitchell," the shrink says. "I would like very much to continue our conversation next week. Would that be amenable to you?"

"Don't have much choice in here do I?" But then I feel bad. After all, she's just a girl, so young. So I add, "Sure, I could talk to you again."

That night in my bunk, I went over everything that was said at the session. You do that when you're in prison. Every thing that's outside of the ordinary routine, you relish and think over and over in your head. I couldn't sleep all that night until the wee hours of the morning. And then I had all these crazy, fast-moving dreams, like spring river water flowing real hard and dizzying. Then the morning guards rattled the bars with their batons and I was awake to the humming institutional lights of Matsqui. The only kind of light I see these days.

The following week, I see her again.

"Hello Carina. How are you?"

She looks up at me but she isn't smiling. Her face is pinched, sore. Concerned maybe? It even looks like she is trying hard not to cry.

"Mitchell, sit down please. Guard, I need one of his arms to be untethered, I have something for him to read, and he must hold it himself. Thank you."

"You got something for me?"

"Yes Mitchell. I won't beat around the bush with this. After we spoke last week, I wanted to do some background research about you. I have a colleague who works in the records department for the provincial social services. She has access to all the old records for wards of the province. I hope you don't mind – you signed a blanket release when you got in here so I asked her to look up your old file from when you were in care as a child. It had a lot of things, she said, but she sent me something really interesting. I thought you might like to read it."

Carina hands me an old yellowed envelope with a letter inside.

"There were others, the file said, but they were destroyed. This one was just kept for 'evidence' – I assume evidence to use against your mother in her quest to regain custody of you."

"It's from my mum?"

"Yes, one of many. The file said she wrote to you every week when you were in reform school, then foster homes. I have to warn you, it broke my heart just reading it... Mitchell..."

I slowly flip the envelope over in my hands, it is so old and fragile now. On the front is a nasty looking large black ink stamp that reads plainly: **CENSORED**. And written in red ink below is the word: *rejected.* Carefully, I lift the flap and take out a neatly folded paper, also yellowed with age. The folds are so worn they have almost given way. And the writing is very faded – it is scrawled in pencil – my mother's handwriting.

Dear Mitchell,
How is my big boy? I miss you lots and lots. Someday soon we will be together again and we will go on a fishing trip up on Quiet Lake. It is a cold winter now so I made you some pairs of wool pants I will send them to you so you can be warm. I still have your Pongy doll here, remember him? Your little bear I made from a potato sack and buttons for eyes. He is waiting for you and I am too. We will see you again really soon. Maybe we could meet at the ferry station in Vancouver? How about I meet you there on Saturday, no next Saturday, enough time for this letter to get to you, and we can see each other then? I'll bring Pongy too. I'll be waiting for the boat that comes in from the Island with you. I'll check every boat. I loves you so much and always will.

Bye, bye my Mitchell.
Love Mummy

"Can I keep it?" I ask a moment later, tears raking down my hardened face.

"Of course you can. It was meant for you all along."

CHAPTER FIFTEEN
Sylvia

I found him listed in the online phone directory on the Internet. I am sitting cross-legged on my bed with the phone in my lap and Zurbeenie is stalking a small spider on the carpet of my room.

"Allo?"

"Um, hi. Is this Pierre Legault?"

"Oui, oo is speaking?"

"This is Sylvia Hardy – your daughter. My mother's name is Miriam Hardy."

Dead silence on the other end of the line. On this end my tense muscles jump as Zurbeenie leaps Superman-style across the floor at the unfortunate spider.

"Sorry to call you up out of the blue like this. I heard that you were working in the Abbotsford area and so I thought I would look you up — "

"You want money? You call for money from me?"

I can't believe he just said that. I can't believe I called him. The absurdity of my romanticized notion of Pierre has me turning red and sweating. Zurbeenie has crunched up the spider and is now making an ungodly sound hacking up fur-balls. It's so loud that I'm sure Pierre can hear it through the phone.

"Well now that you mention it, you got any cash?"

Pierre is quiet again. I guess he didn't pick up on my sarcasm, which I tend to fall back on when I don't know what to say.

"Look Pierre, I'm not after money, I — "

"You call attorney?" This turns out to be more of a question than a demand. Zurbeenie, fully recovered, is now tracking a moth with her eyes. Her head is going up and down, side to side, almost even backwards like an owl's.

"No, no, I don't want anything like that. I was just thinking maybe we could meet or something…"

"My English bad. I have no money to give."

"Sure." I say, then I hang up, mad at myself for taking this so lightly in the first place. Clearly, he still wants nothing to do with me.

Zurbeenie feels some real or imagined poke and jumps straight up in the air, then zooms out of my room so fast she is a blur. I lean over and slam the door shut.

An hour later, Lydie is meeting me for an emergency coffee down on South Kingsway, near her house. I told her what happened over the phone. When she rushes into the donut shop she immediately puts her arms around me and says her there, theres.

"Thanks Lydie."

"Bastard men."

"Yes, that pretty much sums it up."

"You feel better soon. Let's get some food into you."

Against my faltering protests, Lydie buys me a soup and sandwich. I pick at it for a while before saying anything. Lydie never asked, but I feel like I have to explain it.

"I guess I wanted there to be some sort of connection with him or something. Some sort of breakthrough – some long lost 'hey, where have you been all these years?' some recognition or something. But it was like talking to a complete stranger."

Lydie nods her head.

"He is my own biological father but he is a complete stranger. It's like I don't even know who half of me is."

Lydie nods her head again. Strange for her not to say anything. Usually she is full of advice.

"People who grow up knowing their real dads are so lucky." I'm turning bitter now with her lack of response.

Lydie nods again.

"You grew up with your real dad – didn't you?"

"Yes. But then the kids were taken away to residential school and they didn't know their daddies anymore, not like the way they used to. They weren't allowed to speak the language of their daddies and they were taught to hate the ways of their daddies."

"Lydie, do you realize you just answered my question in the third person?"

She shrugs.

"You done picking at that food, skinny girl? I got something make you feel better." Lydie says suddenly.

"What?"

"You have to come outside."

Lydie leads me out the door and around to the back brick wall of the Robins Donuts, in an alley that looks like a refuge for homeless people. She digs through her packsack for a minute then pulls out a small tin. She opens it up and holds it up for me to see. There are two rolled joints inside.

"Lydie! Where the hell did you get those?" I screech.

"Shhh! Jonah's room. He grows some plants and makes his own. He thinks I don't know about it but I'm not stupid."

"Holy shit. Do you do this stuff all the time?"

"No, never. I just thought you need some help to make you forget for a little bit. Come on, I got a lighter from Jonah's room too." Lydie lights up a joint and hands it to me. I don't tell her that I've done it before, on occasion with River. She lights up her own and takes a deep draw. She breaks out coughing and spurts into laughter. I'm thinking this was more for her own amusement than anything.

I take a drag too and the stuff goes to work almost immediately. Damn it feels good to be a little bit light-headed for once these days.

"Thanks, Lydie."

Lydie gabbles on about how her boys tease her for being gullible, but really she's just puts on a show for them. I see some movement behind Lydie and glance over her left shoulder.

A bicycle cop is walking his bike down the alley right toward us.

"Lydie!" I gesture frantically toward to cop. But it's too

late to hide our joints. Lydie turns around and smiles at the approaching cop.

"Good afternoon officer. Me and my girl were just having a nice little smoke here to make her feel better. Her real dad's an asshole." The large cop is staring at me with that blank, authoritative man-stare. All business and no room to even wiggle.

"I'm sorry officer, we've never done this before – it's my fault – I was having a breakdown because I called my real dad and he told me to get a lawyer and – it's just one little joint, well two actually — "

Lydie cuts in. "Where your manners girl? Offer the man a toke."

I am speechless at her audacity.

She shakes her head as though she is exasperated with my lack of manners and offers her joint to the cop. He stares at it for a minute, then takes it delicately between his two large fingers and inhales deeply.

"Locally grown," Lydie says. The cop looks at it, nods, and hands it back to her.

"You girls hurry it along."

"Yes sir, officer," Lydie chimes as the cop turns on his heel and lumbers his bicycle out of the alley.

As soon as he is out of earshot, Lydie bursts out laughing.

"Jeez m'girl, you should see the look on your face!"

"Lydie!"

"Come on now, Sylvie-girl. Do you think he would arrest a sweet old lady like me?"

Later that night, the weed and the uncomfortable encounter with my real dad must have been messing with my head. I wake up in a sweat about this weird dream I had. Nothing scary, just one of those disturbing little-kid dreams. I was back in primary school again and it was pizza day. For some reason all the kids took turns paying for everyone's pizza in the dream, and that day it was my turn. There I was at school and I had forgotten to bring the money for pizza day. The only thing I could think of was to call my mom and ask her to bake pizzas for all the kids. But then I couldn't remember her goddamn phone number. I had it written down on a piece of paper, but I couldn't read the writing so I just kept dialling the wrong number and the kids were getting hungrier and angrier and all I could do was just keep dialling, but the call never went through to my mother.

Frigging weird dream. But it reminds me of how things were. In fact, I bet I can trace the dream back to an event that did actually happen. At least I think it did. After Tommy was taken, I tried to forget so much.

I must have been in high school by then because my homeroom class was embarking on a field trip to a museum in Calgary. My mom was supposed to give me the thirty dollars that day for the admission fee, bus ride, and lunch money, but she told me she forgot all about it. And now she was broke. I asked her where my monthly allowance went and she said she spent it on some expensive mail-order revitalizing eye serum. Even now I remember just looking at her dumbfounded. The look on my face provoked a reaction.

"Well, do you want me to get old and wrinkled and look like a hag? Get a job and get your own money. You can't always count on me to bail you out – I'm teaching you a good life lesson here."

What is a teenaged girl to do in response to that? I screamed at her that I was dropping out of school. I even stayed home in the smoke-infested, Boxcar Huey-reeking house for three whole days to show her I was serious. I got pretty good grades so it killed me to stay home and to think of all the schoolwork piling up on my empty desk. My mother just sat in her chair, smoking and watching her soap operas, and she never paid any attention to me. Even when I would make a point of stomping by her through the living room, she didn't so much as flinch, let alone try to get me to go back to school. The only interaction she had during the day was when Boxcar Huey emerged from his room and needed her to open another bottle for him. Of course she took some for herself too, saying it was payment for him living there for free.

Then, on the third day, Mr. Tomlinson, the guidance counselor and part-time truancy officer from school, came by. I remember standing in the bathroom and straining to hear through the door what my mother would say.

"Sylvia does her own thing. She doesn't listen to me. You know how adolescent girls are." Her voice had no trace of anger that I could detect, rather, it was quite glib. Really, she couldn't have cared less.

I burst out of the bathroom door and marched down the hall.

"Fine then. I'm going back to school. Does that make you happy? Then I won't have to see your ugly, wrinkly face around here everyday!"

"Fine with me, missy," she said looking down at me, then mouthing something I couldn't decipher behind her hand to Mr. Tomlinson. Mr. Tomlinson asked if he could speak to her alone outside. I peeked through the curtains in the kitchen window and I could see them smiling and laughing outside. Mr. Tomlinson even put his hand on my mother's shoulder at one point. For that brief moment, out there on the driveway, my mother came alive again. Then, when Mr. Tomlinson was walking back to his car, he looked up at me in the window and saluted me yelling, "See ya at school, Scout!"

When my mother came in I pounced on her immediately and asked her what they were talking about and what was so funny.

But I could see her already retreating, and the sound of me, my voice, made her retreat even more. She became that ghost in the house once again. Present, but not really there. She didn't answer me. Perhaps she was not purposely ignoring me; perhaps she merely couldn't break through her wall of pain and elusiveness to answer me. She had gone to some strange place of ambiguity that the mind of the grieving falls into.

She simply exhaled, eyes blank, her body brushing past me to return to her television shows.

CHAPTER SIXTEEN
Pierre

He was bothered by the phone call, but not bothered enough to do anything about it. He thought she sounded a lot like Miriam had, back when she was in her early twenties and not yet so bitter. But Miriam is older now, late forties, and a lot has changed since then. The girl – Sylvia, the oldest one – had that thing in her voice that Miriam once had. The teasing just below the surface, the fun even through the hurt. She said she had not wanted anything, but he could read her better than she knew. Miriam used to say she didn't want anything either. Just his body on top of hers and the fashionable dresses he used to buy her.

Miriam was just a child when he met her, barely eighteen, and he was a good ten years older – closer to twelve actually. He had lied about his age at first and so had she. One day, as she sat in the cab of his truck while he was refuelling, she snooped through his wallet and found the truth printed on his Quebec driver's license. Miriam had a fit, a raging tantrum, and made him beg and cry for forgiveness, because by then he was already hooked on her. The scent of her skin, the sight of her upper legs, bare and white, wrapped around him. He thought he couldn't live without her, or the physicality of her. So when she had brought him right to the brink of pleading for mercy, as much as any man could, she dropped her own bomb right down on him. She was not twenty-three. Not really. But she was legal to vote and mature for her age.

He first met her when he was on a temporary field assignment in Calgary. He was only there for six months, mapping geological hazards west of the city, but after he met Miriam at a nightclub he signed on to stay with the project for another year so he could explore and delve into this curiously fresh sexual creature some more.

She was ferocious for one so young and her long auburn hair flew about her as she moved, those incredible legs taking her places very quickly. She would often just bust out and dance right there on the street while they waited for a taxi after drinking all evening. And she would pull him to her, and he always obliged her. Onlookers stared as their hips and pelvis ground into one another, and he didn't care. He couldn't get enough of her, the taste of her. *Miriam.*

She still lived with her parents in Medicine Hat then, but they were passive and not too concerned with the whereabouts of their four young daughters. It was the swinging Seventies, after all. Miriam spent a lot of time with Pierre in Calgary at his flat, where they made love on every stick of furniture in the place, including the large cabinet-style television. It seemed like they were always screwing or eating, and they did so with great relish and desire.

The passionate, unprotected sex led to a pregnancy, and then a baby. Soon after Miriam found out she was pregnant again. Two children, barely two years apart. Things seemed to be getting away from them faster than they could digest. Pierre tried to provide, but Miriam changed after the birth of the girls. She became increasingly hysterical, morose, and uninterested in sex. He now recognizes that she was most likely suffering from postpartum depression.

They did not think about that back then. Miriam had no allies and she resented Pierre for what she was going through, even though neither one of them understood what it was. She did not know that he fantasized every night that she was still an eighteen-year-old, back when he was the only man who had been with her. Now that she had been pried into by old men doctors and strange, squalling beings had been brought forth out of her, she was not the same young doll Pierre had once possessed. She was becoming something else entirely, something that was no longer attractive to him. And if he couldn't have what he had been staying here for, then there was nothing else to do but leave. She was driving him away anyhow.

On the day he left, he wrote a letter to Miriam to remind her of how things used to be. He put seven hundred dollars in cash in an envelope and taped it to the fridge where she would be sure to see it. The apartment lease was up in three months so she could stay until then. After that she would have to return to live with her mother, two kids in tow. The thought of that made Pierre wince. He had transformed an exotic, beautiful, sensual creature into a haggard, depressed, penniless, single mother. And he hated himself for that. He could never look back on those years spent in Alberta.

Pierre moved back to Quebec, back to his family home. Miriam called once to scream at him but only that once. One time Pierre sent a check and he waited and waited for a response. But a full year passed, and the check was never cashed or deposited. He stopped sending letters and money after that.

He sometimes still wondered about the girls – who they look like, who they take after. But he would never dream of contacting them because he was convinced they had been taught to hate him for being absent, and he was right. That day when the oldest one called, Sylvia, it confused him and shook him up. He thought briefly about pulling up stakes again from Abbotsford and moving back East, where he would have put enough distance behind him and the family he almost had out West. But in this day and age of the Internet, it would be too easy for any of them to track him down. He decided to just forget about it and stay where he was. Maybe he scared her off enough with his lack of conversation and the distance in his voice. It was only a very brief phone call. She had hung up on *him* after all, not he on her. Perhaps that little phone call glitch was only that, a little glitch.

CHAPTER SEVENTEEN
Lydie

That poor girl Sylvia. Her real daddy abandoned her, and her mummy won't talk to her no more. I try to mind my own business about it, but it's hard for me. I wish I could have Sylvia as my daughter. Then she wouldn't be going around feeling like she hate herself. Sometimes I think maybe Sylvia is my daughter who died when she was a baby. Maybe she come back as a white girl to teach me some lesson. Or for me to teach her some lesson. I don't believe in coincidences. I think everything happens for some reason. Even the bad stuff in life.

I tell my boys growing up about the bad things that happen at residential school. Lots of old folks don't talk about it, but here's what I think: good to talk it out of the soul and teach people what we went through so maybe it won't happen again. I tell my boys about how we Indian kids fought back, how we wiggled our toes under the blankets when the mean dorm matrons screamed at us not to move another muscle. I talk about how the kids were separated, boys on one side, girls on the other, but how we always found ways to meet and talk to one another. Like flying paper airplanes with secret notes written in codes over the partition that divided us. It is hard to keep families apart when they love each other. I tell Sylvia about this too so she knows that even if a person is in a bad place, as long as they love someone then they can get through it. That's why I don't worry about my Mitchell in the correctional institute. I know he gets fed and a warm place to sleep and I know he knows he has a mummy who loves him. Because I tell him all the time when he allowed to make phone calls. And he tell me he going to change. My Mitchell wants to do better.

Jonah I worry about, though. Last couple years, he drinking too much like his Old Man. I find him drunk a lot after he come home from work at the mechanic shop, and sometimes early as noontime. Jonah and I watch the news sometimes at night and see many sad things. He says life is just too tragic and he feels it's so hard to be a Native person in this life in modern days. He wishes for the olden days that he never even knew about – they were long before his time. He say he know why all those kids today kill themselves up in the remote northern reserves. Just too much hopelessness and no one to help them see out of it, because all the grown-ups are hopeless too.

This morning Jonah tell me about a dream he had last night. He tell me that he go to many doors in many neighborhoods all over Canada and stand and knock at the doors but could never go in. He just look into the windows and see the life going on in there but he not allowed in. All he could do was just stand there all by himself, lonely outside the door. And never be allowed inside. He make me cry when he tell his dream.

Once I went to an Al-Anon meeting because a counselor at the university Longhouse suggested it. It was just for family members of people who are alcoholics, and the Creator knows, I've had a lot of them in my long life. There were all kinds of people there at the meeting, too many for everyone to be able to talk, so I just listened. Lots of talk about enabling stuff and they explained all about that. I didn't really understand it back then, but sometimes I think about it now and wonder if I do that for Jonah. But how could that be a bad thing? I could never turn my back on him, especially when he need me so bad. He was taken away too young from his mummy, and just like a pup who is weaned too early, he will need extra care for the rest of his life. But I understand he still needs to stand on his own. I have him go sometimes and talk to elders and do sweats and healing ceremonies and he says that really helps. But still he drinks. The crazy water sure has a tight hold of him and I don't know what to do about it, 'cept to love him harder.

This morning I go to UBC campus to meet up with my Canadian History class one last time. We are going on little field trip to see some guns and stuff. Probably will be just a small group of the class since it's 8:30 in the morning and our final grades have already been handed in so we can graduate on time. Most of the kids not worry about getting out of bed so early today and most of them don't like Professor Gooch anyways. But I like to be outside early in the morning. The sun is really orange from the east and it covers over things just beautifully in the early morning hours. Green grass is shimmering from all the dew. The mountains to the north are red and purple in the morning light. Ocean water in the Burrard Inlet is twinkling and winking at me. I am the first one to meet at the Museum of Anthropology, besides the professor.

Good day, Lydie Jim, Professor Gooch says. Happy morning I tell him and we chat about the sunshine and springtime. A couple more students show up – the smart ones or the ones who really into history. Professor Gooch is disappointed that only five people wanted to come on his end-of-class field trip but he said, that's okay, it more fun with a smaller group. He teach Canadian history but his special area, he always tell us, is in war history. He a tall, fat man with hardly any hair and a big red face. He lead us over behind the Museum of Anthropology and show us some big round platform of cement with part of old iron railing and many big, rusty bolts in the middle. This, he tell us, is the remnants of a Mk7 gun that was mounted here during World War II – now it is a memorial but there used to be three mounted right here on this site in the 1940s aimed out toward Japan. He then take us over to some bushes and push through the leaves right inside the stand of trees, muttering to himself. The other students looking at each other like he crazy. He stomp aside ferns and tall grass until he find what he looking for. There is a big, rusted metal door welded shut right in the side of a hill – just like a tunnel into the earth.

This here is the entrance to one of the only remaining bunkers, Professor Gooch tell us. Used to be that you could go inside here and run around in the underground tunnels but the university put the kibosh to that a few years back. He tell us that these tunnels were bunkers and bomb shelters during World War II because Point Grey, where the university stands, is perfect spot for lookout for enemy boats and submarines. I can tell that Professor Gooch is really excited by all this old war stuff, but not so much me.

Sometimes I think back to that time, and I can remember it – not like all these young people today who are so new to history. No, I can remember when we heard up in Teslin that a war had started again over the big ocean, and Canada was going to send men to fight there. Used to be in the old treaties that Native people didn't have to go to war for Britain – at the time Canada was still part of Britain – but all that changed by the year 1940 and most Native people were not exempt from the conscription anymore. But most Native people never complained, they just did it bravely for pride of being a warrior – like my Samuel – he volunteered early on and traveled down to the Lower Mainland to join up with the army. And he volunteered to go over the sea to fight in the front of the line battles. That's where he got killed – my Samuel – early on in the war. We was married a year before he left and we had a baby girl together, Gracie was her name. Samuel kissed us good-bye before he get on the train at Whitehorse and promised he would be back. But he get killed, it said in the government letter that the policemen delivered to me. And it said they buried his body over there across the seas in some field. That was the most heartache I ever felt at the time and I thought I would die from losing my husband Samuel. But I didn't. And more heartache was to come, lots more, when my little Gracie drownded in the river. And so much more hurting through the years on this poor heart, all through my life. But I learned how to live with it and I hope it make me a better person.

Professor Gooch then take us hiking down to the beach. Two nice young students hold my elbows because I'm old and need help over the rocks and logs. Professor Gooch point out old remains of searchlight towers from the war where long-haired, half-naked hippies now camp out. They painted peace signs and flowers all over the ugly towers. Professor Gooch shake his head, mad about what the hippies did, and tell us these towers are monuments to Canada's military past and should be treated with great respect and admiration. I say to the young boy standing next to me that they look more like a monument to the flower-power people!

After Professor Gooch say we are dismissed, I walk back through the yard of the Museum of Anthropology and look up at the totem poles. I wonder why Professor Gooch only sees the military history of this place when there has been so much else. He never mentioned the Musqueam people who lived here many hundreds of years before the Canadian military ever came here looking for enemy boats.

Later today I knock at Sylvia's door. We have just a couple more things we need to work on with our final papers for Literature class. Then it will be time for graduation.

Sylvie girl, it's a happy day outside. Nature singing your name, I tell her.

She say, (bad word) Lydie, how can you always be so optimistic? She strumming some song on her little guitar, kicking the cat with the funny name to leave her alone from rubbing on her leg.

I tell her, wash your mouth out with soap, girl! And look out the window. The sky is smiling. Hopefully the sunshine comes to visit us on graduation day.

Sylvia says, yes, that would be nice.

Then I ask her if her mummy coming to see her graduate?

Sylvia is quiet for a minute, only strumming more loudly and harder on the little guitar. She scares kitty with the funny name right out of the room.

No, Lydie, she says, I didn't invite her. And even if I did, she wouldn't come. You know she hates my guts.

I tell her, that's not right, m'girl. A mummy should never hate her own daughter. Maybe she just confused about who she mad at.

Oh no, Sylvia says. She has made it clear that ever since Tommy disappeared it was my fault because I was supposed to be babysitting him.

But you didn't take Tommy and hurt him.

Sylvia quiet for a minute, playing softer now on her little guitar. Then says, no but my mother still thinks it wouldn't have happened if I had been outside in the yard with him, rather than inside talking on the phone.

Yes, but then if you were outside, your mummy might have lost two kids that day, not just one, I tell her.

Sylvia is quiet again. No guitar sounds now. She put it down on the floor beside her. I can see her thoughts hurt inside of her.

What do you think? I ask her.

I think…I think the whole thing is fucked up, she says. I think my mother was always fragile and that just sent her over the edge. Losing Tommy. She had a hard life before that too.

You know girl, when I came back from residential school I wasn't a girl no more and it was hard for me to be the same around my mummy. We couldn't even talk the same language anymore. She forgot her English and I forgot a lot of our own languages. And my daddy was dead by then. But we still loved each other, Mummy and me. We could still sing the song together over Quiet Lake, just like when I was a little girl.

Well that's nice, Sylvia says. There won't be no singing of songs for me and my mother.

Maybe you should call your mummy and invite her to graduation.

Sylvia turn and look at me and say: Lydie, maybe you should mind your own business – look, it's a painful thing and I just have to go on in life without her. Because she'll never get past her anger. I don't blame her for it – I mean her little boy got kidnapped and murdered! Where does a parent go after that? How can you go on living? I understand that her anger at me is a way to cope with a horrendous loss. It is messed up I know, but there's no righting this one. End of story.

Just then Sylvia's roommate pokes her head in and asks Sylvia to help her unload some groceries from her car. Since I am an old lady, she doesn't ask me to help. Here I am, left alone in Sylvia's room.

My eyes start to look around and I wonder…I wonder

where Sylvia would keep her address book. My hand feels its way over to a drawer in a table beside the bed and there's nothing but magazines, box of Twinkies, and a mystery novel in there. Then I shuffle my old lady feet over to Sylvia's desk and…bingo! There is an address book in the top drawer. I flip it open to the H section and see the name *Miriam Hardy*. It doesn't say mum but I know this is Sylvia's mum's name because she always calls her by Miriam. I scribble down her mummy's phone number and sit back down to pretend like I wasn't up to no sneaky stuff.

CHAPTER EIGHTEEN
Jonah

I find Sylvia's phone number in my mother's address book, which is always lying around the house. I don't really know what I am going to say to Ms. Sylvia, but I feel like I owe her at least a phone call.

She answers right away.

"Hey Sylvia, it's Jonah. I wanted to say sorry for the other day. That was kind of awkward." I get it all out in one sentence.

After a pause she replies, "Yeah, it wasn't very pleasant, was it?"

"I'm sorry. Sometimes...well, you know."

"Yeah. Whatever, eh?"

It is pretty obvious that she is pissed-off at me. And I don't blame her.

"Listen, I am going to this whaling festival up on the Northwest coast this weekend. I thought maybe it would be something you'd find interesting."

"Are you drunk?"

"No."

"But you've been drinking?"

"No, I swear – I just wanted to invite you to the whaling festival."

"Are you *kidding me?* Whale hunting? As in slaughtering massive sea mammals and then carving them up with chainsaws on the beach and spilling their guts out?" Sylvia screeches. I can tell already this was a bad idea.

"It's not exactly like that."

"I watch the news Jonah – I have seen the footage."

"The media is so slanted about the issue. They really sensationalize the whole Native whaling thing."

"The whole thing is clearly barbaric no matter if it is white men or aboriginal men doing the killing – excuse me – 'harvesting' as they call it."

"What are you talking about? The coastal Native people have been harvesting whales since the beginning of time. It's more than just a food source for them – it's a cultural right of passage."

"Sorry, but I don't think any human being has the right to take a life like that."

"Oh come on, Sylvia! You eat hamburgers, don't you? And sushi? How do you think those things end up on your plate?"

"My point is that it is ludicrous and human-centric that people of any kind think they have a right to slaughter – in the most cruel way – other creatures in the name of 'cultural' pursuits."

I don't know what keeps me going on this subject with her, but there is something…entertaining about it.

"Now Sylvia, that's a bit culturally insensitive, don't you think? Are you saying that Native people are being selfish and cruel in their quest to reclaim their cultural identities? Isn't that sort of racist?"

"I am not being racist! Jonah, quit twisting my words!"

I have to suppress a chuckle. But I know when to stop. I've pushed her to about as far as she can go.

"Well how about coming up the coast with me this weekend and you can see for yourself what goes on? How about it Sylvia?"

"Jonah! No! Absolutely not. Is this funny to you?"

"Well, just a little. But I am serious about the offer. Just trying to be a good guy."

There is no response from her for a few seconds. So I go ahead and fill the silence.

"Okay, I see that I am being turned down here. I thought it would be worth a try."

"Well I'm glad I am worth the effort." Sylvia laughs wryly, then hangs up the phone on me.

After listening to the blaring dial tone for a minute, I place Lydie's address book in the same spot where I found it. *I really fucked that up.*

I'm sure Sylvia will mention the phone call to Lydie, and maybe even ask her what it was all about. If – or I should say *when* – Lydie asks me about calling Sylvia, I don't know how I will respond. I don't even really know myself why I called her.

I really got under Sylvia's skin.

But, it was good to hear her voice.

CHAPTER NINETEEN
Sylvia

I was feeling raw and pensive after Jonah's call, so perhaps River was not the best person for me to be around at the time. He was conversational and kept trying to engage me, but I was quietly lost in my own world of gnarled-up emotion and bewildering thoughts. River hadn't brought up the question of our moving in together in recent days, but I could tell he was itching to ask me. I hadn't quite thought of an appropriate answer yet.

When our wild salmon and wild rice dinner was all but licked clean from our plates, River had a strange request. He wanted to interview me for his research proposal to get into graduate school. It is not due for another half a year, but of course, all River thinks about is his post-modernist plight and his duty to bring forth his ruminations into the world. Turns out he wasn't interested in me personally, but in Boxcar Huey. I had told River amusing stories about him on previous occasions. River is fascinated with homeless people, the downtrodden, the poor. He wanted to tape me talking about Boxcar Huey.

"What kind of stuff do you want to know? I already told you everything there is to know."

"Well, the gentleman's background for one, or what you know of it; how he became an alcoholic, homeless; was there some pivotal event in his early years? I mean, who really was the man behind that bedroom door? Don't you ever wonder?" The excitement in River's voice mounted.

"Not really. It's a stretch to call him a 'gentleman.' He was just a drunk old guy my mom felt sorry for. He was related to her, you know. Distantly."

"Yes, but what would motivate your mother to take in a homeless guy to live in her house – with her children, no less! Who does that sort of thing?"

"Like I said, he was a relative of hers or something. Isn't that motivation enough?"

"There has to be something else worth digging for. Something more than just a distant cousin, decades older than her, and whom she didn't really know."

"Maybe she just wanted the free booze and his old-age pension check so she didn't have to go out and work herself. I'm sure it's nothing fantastically mind-boggling like you are supposing." River was really annoying me at this point.

"Well then, Sylvia, have you ever asked yourself this: if your mother had enough benevolence and compassion to take in a near stranger – chronically inebriated and hygieni-cally challenged as you describe him – then why on earth would she shun her own daughter?"

"I do not know the answer to that, River. But I do know that you can really be *soooo* asinine sometimes."

That was yesterday. Last exam is today. Many, many things are swimming frantically around in my brain – bits of emotional conversations, unresolved feelings with no descriptive words – I just have to put all the brain-clog aside for now. My full attention has to be on this final exam. The last one of four years of undergraduate work. Then it's graduation and I am done. I will have my Bachelor of Arts degree in psychology with a minor in literature. Yay! Then I will be done with it. And on to the next phase of my life. What that will shape up to be, I have no idea.

But for now, one more exam. I am running a little late this morning trying to get my hair smoothed down. I wash it at night so Mui and I aren't competing for the shower in the morning and sometimes I wake up with a gigantic cowlick in the back of my head. The darn thing won't settle down today, so I grab a beret from my closet shelf and stuff my puffy hair in that. I snatch my packsack and rush out the door to the bus stop. I've already missed the 7:15 bus and I am close to missing the 7:25. My exam is at 9:00 sharp. It takes almost an hour on the bus to get to campus in the morning rush hour, then another fifteen minutes to walk to the auditorium where the exam will be held.

So much for being early to cram in some last-minute studying. In years past, I used to come a full two hours early and sit with all the other nerds, pouring over my books for some desperate intellectual breakthrough before the exam. Now I will be lucky if I make it there before they lock the doors.

When it comes, the bus is absolutely jam-packed with all the other students and Westside morning commuters, who are mainly housekeeping staff for the large mansions that flank the university grounds. Everyone is damp or dripping from the rainy morning and to compensate, the bus driver has the heat turned on full blast, even though it is late April. The hot air cooks us and the stench from soggy umbrellas and wet sneakers is unbearable. I am sweating profusely inside my layers of sweaters and from the wool beret. I know that my armpits are drenched, but now I can feel beads of perspiration breaking out on my top lip and my nose. My breathing becomes shaky and uneven and my head starts to feel like it is buzzing. I feel like I might pass out. Or vomit. Even though there are people all around me, no one seems to notice my distress.

I bend down into a squatting position. Even though my head is really close to someone's behind, I have to rest it on my arm, which is clasped desperately around a pole, sweaty palm and all. My vision is going in and out of focus so I can only intermittently see people staring at me. I concentrate on trying to get air into my lungs. As long as I can keep breathing, I might be able to stay upright. Then my stomach starts to turn. I can feel the throw-up forming in my belly and I'm getting that weird kneading feeling in my stomach. The bus lurches to a stop and as two people get on, I push my way out the back doors and fall down in the wet grass just beyond the sidewalk. The fumes from the idling bus do me in and I vomit on the grass.

God help me, I think. Then, *Jonah where are you when I need you?*

After the bus pulls away and the air clears somewhat of pollutants, I start to feel better. But I am really shaky and I don't think I can stand up just yet. I wonder why my mind is summoning Jonah for strength – right after God, whom I really don't even believe in. *What the hell is wrong with me lately?*

Then I remember my exam. And that was the last bus that would get me there on time. I start stumbling along the wet sidewalk, not even caring about the slugs and the worms. My head is lolling around like I am drunk and my mouth is open, trying to suck in some oxygen.

Then, a female voice beside me. "Sylvia! Hey! Need a ride? I'm heading that way for work."

I look over at a gray car pulled up beside me. It's Julie, Mui's long-time girlfriend. I have seen her driving this route before, so I know it is not totally a divine intervention.

"Yes! Please! Thank you, Julie! I am going to be late for my exam." I climb in the passenger side and nod at Julie appreciatively, thinking to myself, *You idiot, praying for God or Jonah, and it's a lesbian who bails you out in the end.*

Julie expertly maneuvers around traffic and takes some short cuts on campus – even where no cars are allowed – and gets me to the exam auditorium just as the last of the anxious students are shuffling their way inside.

"Thanks, Julie. You saved my academic life. I owe you a beer, or a kiss, or something."

Inside the auditorium, papers shuffle and a hundred quiet murmurs can be heard before the head professor calls for silence. I line up all my pencils for the multiple-choice section. My hands are still sweating but my breathing has become steady now. I really stink from perspiring. I hope the people next to me cannot smell it. I place the bottle of water Julie gave me beside my pencils and try to clear my head, focus my brain. But I keep thinking of Boxcar Huey. Then Jonah. Then Boxcar Huey. *Why the hell Boxcar Huey? Why Jonah?* The exam instructions and papers are handed out. Then the clock is set and the exam begins.

The following day I am meeting with Lydie down at Stanley Park. We both decided that things were getting a little too stressful and intense so we thought we would do something fun today. Besides, we are both done all of our exams. Now it's time for some relaxation and celebration.

She said to wait by the horse wagon kiosk and she would be there by 11:45. I glance at my watch and see that it is already noon and there's still no sign of Lydie. That's not like her. Usually, she is early. I start to worry.

Then I see a tall, longhaired Native guy in jeans coming toward me with deliberate, powerful strides. Jonah. Wouldn't ya know it?

"What, is Lydie trying to set us up on a blind date or something? You know I already have a boyfriend. And you seem to have no shortage of lady friends."

Jonah closes his eyes briefly and shakes his head. "No, Lydie got sick with the stomach flu and I guess you had already left your house when she tried to call you. She sent me to tell you so you wouldn't be waiting here all day and worrying." I catch a whiff of his breath. He smells like alcohol already and it is only lunchtime.

"Well that was thoughtful of her. I had a touch of the stomach flu myself the other day. Maybe it's going around."

"Yeah that happens…now that I'm here, do you want to grab something to eat?"

"You sure are determined Jonah. And persistent. Are you buying? Is this like a date? Don't you be thinking that I'll end up in the sack quite so quick like what's-her-name. What *is* her name?"

Jonah narrows his eyes at me and gives me that head-shake thing again.

"Wish that wouldn't have happened. Regret it." Jonah says quietly.

"Regret what? That I saw you with her, or that you slept with her?"

"Both. I'm sorry, okay? Now can we get over it and eat?"

"As long as whale meat is not on the menu."

I get the feeling that I have given Jonah enough flogging for his indiscretions. He really does seem to feel bad about it.

We agree on chili cheese dogs at a nearby stand and we sit on some large rocks overlooking the water. Jonah orders a soda. Maybe that'll get rid of the beer smell. Or maybe he is the kind of chronic alcoholic who just emanates alcohol through his pores. Like Boxcar Huey.

"Don't you have to go back to work today?" I quiz him.

"Took the rest of the day off." Jonah says, chomping on his chili dog.

"Am I that special?" I tease.

"Actually, the boss brought some beer in this morning and the guys started playing poker with the boss and then he shut the shop down for the afternoon. We didn't have enough work for the full crew anyway. So I left."

I notice that Jonah has a leaf tangled in his hair, which is tied back in a ponytail. My hand is just an inch away from running through his hair to extricate the leaf when he grabs my wrist with the speed and force of a robotic device.

"Whoa, man! I was just going to pull a leaf out of your hair."

"In my culture it is rude to touch a man's hair. A person's hair has a lot of power and it is a very personal thing. You can't just walk up to an Indian guy and play with his hair like he's some poodle." I can't tell if he is serious or pulling my leg again.

"Oh sure, but a sleazy woman can go around grabbing your ass and sucking on your face," I shoot back – and regret it as soon as the words leave my mouth.

His response is non-verbal. His face appears tired, sad, and old. The anger is gone. Only regret once again. His mood seems different today than the other day on the phone.

"Jeez, Jonah. I meant no disrespect. Sorry. I didn't know it was such a big deal to you – your hair."

"Now you know. You done? Come on, let's walk on the seawall."

Feeling like an admonished child, I hop along beside Jonah, hoping to make things better between us.

"You do have nice hair though, Jonah. It suits you."

He just nods and smiles.

"Where's your boyfriend today, Sylvia?"

"Why does everyone ask me that? Like I'm supposed to be wrapped around his arm all the time. He's at work. He does inventory once a month for an organic produce store."

"You in love with him?"

"Maybe. I don't know. If love is just a comfortable,

boring, going-along-with-it feeling, then I guess we are in love. Sometimes he pisses me off, though. With his big ideas and hypocritical intellectual talk. And the way he analyzes me. We've been together for a few years now so I'm used to him. In some ways we are a lot alike – we like the same things, have pretty decent cerebral conversations. I guess that's what I thought a relationship should be."

"What you *thought?* That doesn't sound very convincing. Maybe you should look outside the nest."

"What do you mean by that?"

"Nothing. It just seems like he is a safe choice for you. But meanwhile, maybe you are stuck in some slow-moving quicksand and you don't even realize it."

"Huh. Thanks for the insight Jonah. What about you? How come you're still living with your mom and not married or into something more serious than a one-night-stand?"

"I haven't always lived with my mom. Actually, I was in a relationship when I was a lot younger, real young. Lived with a gal – Gina. She was from northern Manitoba, living in Winnipeg. I moved down there and we were together for a long time. We were going to get married at one time. Even bought her a ring. That's how serious it was."

I realize at this point that Jonah has now dropped his inhibitions and insecurities with me. He is being serious, honest. I know I am experiencing a glimpse of the internal Jonah, the real unguarded Jonah. He trusts me. And I haven't been fair to him.

"Is she the one you had your daughter with?"

"Yeah. Gracie. I named her Gracie, my daughter. After the baby my mother lost before I was even born – my sister.

And Gina gave her the name Athena. So Gracie Athena was her name. It's dumb. We were just kids, not even eighteen."

"That's not dumb. That's a beautiful name – so…I don't know, gracious."

"She was, she was. Far too good for us as parents. We didn't know what the hell we were doing."

"Well what happened?"

"Drugs. Drugs got in the way of everything and pretty much took over. Social services got involved and took our kid away. We were too strung-out to really do anything about it, so they ended up adopting our daughter out permanently. I guess she is still in Manitoba – my daughter. I don't know where she ended up. Gina overdosed a few years back. Died. We went our own ways before that, though. I ended up going to jail for robbery so I didn't have contact with her for a few years. It's my fault. I let it all get away from me."

"Wow, Jonah. I'm sorry. That's some hard living. Hard-luck story," I mumble, unsure of how much sympathy with which to respond. I feel like we are really having an open, soulful moment. I don't want him to shut down – not now.

"Life ain't no fairy tale," he says and that profound sadness comes over his face again. There is something moving and authentic about him, beyond the teasing and the flirting. As much as I delight in the happy Jonah, I like this other side of him too.

Jonah and I silently wander along, kicking stones, nodding to the elderly couples who smile at us as they shuffle by. We keep going further on around the sea wall until we approach the halfway point. We've been walking for two hours now and my feet are beginning to blister in my plastic sandals. Jonah says he knows a shortcut to get to the other side of Stanley Park so we duck onto a trail that leads us into the dense rainforest bush. It is a gorgeous day – we are shaded nicely from the warm sun that peeks through cedars and a cool wind is coming in gently off the ocean, billowing through the redwoods.

"Jonah, how come you never tried to get your daughter back?"

"I told you, I was strung out on drugs."

"No I mean, later, when you got out of jail, or even now? I bet it's not too late. You could probably go to court and get some type of visitation or something."

Jonah breathes in hard and lifts his eyes skyward. "Sylvia, she's gone. All grown up. I'd be a stranger now. And how could I ever face her after I lost her in the first place? It's my fault, and I have to live with it for the rest of my life."

A silence falls between us, and I think I might have hurt Jonah. But I didn't mean to. I just need some help to find answers of my own.

"Jonah, did you know that I had a little brother who went missing?"

"No, I didn't know that." His attention focuses back on me.

"Yeah, Tommy. He was two years old – two and a half actually. He was a real sweetheart. He was just learning how to talk and he loved to give big wet kisses with his tongue sticking out. Anyway, one day when we were visiting my aunt Blanche in Calgary, my mom left me in charge of Tommy and my sister Jessie – I was thirteen and my sister was about eleven. Mom and Aunt Blanche were out shopping at the mall and I was playing outside with Tommy. Jessie had a cold, so she was inside watching television. The phone rang and I went in the house to answer it. I almost took Tommy inside with me but he was having so much fun playing in the mud puddles in Aunt Blanche's driveway, that I left him there. I thought I'd just be a minute. Anyway, I answered the phone and it was this bill collector who was after my mom and he had tracked her down because she used my aunt's address for something. He started saying all this stuff like my mom could end up in jail if she didn't pay some money on the credit card and I started arguing with him. I finally hung up, but it was about ten minutes later. When I went out to get Tommy, he was gone."

"He was gone?"

"He just vanished. I got Jessie and we ran up and down the street looking for him. I didn't know what to do so I called the mall where my mom was at and had her paged. By the time she and Aunt Blanche got home, it was an hour later. Aunt Blanche finally called the police and it took them another hour to get there. Then everything just kind of snowballed from there. Search parties were formed and they fanned out over the neighborhood and the fields beyond, it went on for weeks – and nothing."

"They never found your brother?"

"No. Well, not at the time. For two years he was just gone. Missing. Then, during the summer of 1986, two hikers found some little bones up in the Badlands of Alberta. Investigators went in and recovered the partial skeleton of a young male child. We got the call that it might be Tommy but it took a few months before they could give us a positive identification. Then, yeah, they said it was Tommy. They used old x-rays of his facial bones taken when he had reconstructive surgery for his cleft palate to compare to the remains. The 'maxilla' – that was the piece they found. I still remember hearing about Tommy's little disfigured maxilla. It was the only way they could get a positive ID on him – that and the fragments of his clothing found near the bones. They didn't have DNA technology available back then. So it was all because of his cleft palate that they could tell it was him. The coroner couldn't determine a cause of death from the bones that were found. But obviously it was foul play – he was found so far away from where he went missing, it wasn't a wild animal or anything like that. Obviously, someone had taken him there."

"And killed him?"

"Yeah, killed him. But they could never tell us how he died or even name any suspects. There was this one woman – a witness – she thought she had seen a man who she thought looked like a convicted sex offender with what she *thought* was a young boy riding in the car. But she couldn't give even a halfway good description, or even remember what color the car was. So possibly it was a sexual predator. That would be my guess. The case is still unsolved. They still have Tommy's bones in a box somewhere in storage. In case there are any new breaks or any new pieces of him found."

"Your family never had a funeral for him?"

"Uh no. Come to think of it, we never did. For the two years he was missing, we just hoped he was still alive. There were vigils held for him. Then when the bones were found and identified, the investigation was still ongoing.

He's dead and gone but none of us were ever the same. My mom stopped talking to me. She just got all quiet and steely – never yelled at me or hit me – just closed up to me like a clamshell. At the time, I figured it was her way of coping with everything, but she kept it up until I left home. She still doesn't really talk to me."

"She blames you for what happened to Tommy?"

"I think so. Because I left him outside that day."

"Maybe she blames herself too."

"Who knows what goes on in her head. She's messed-up, that's for sure. She drinks and smokes too much and she'll probably die of lung cancer sitting in her recliner. Her chair that she used to sit in with Tommy. It's all ripped and stained now, armrests worn away. But she never washes it. She wouldn't dream or replacing it. She doesn't really work or do much of anything except hang out with one of my other aunts at the corner store in the neighborhood where she grew up and still lives."

"Your mother is a bitch for being that way. I'm sorry for you Sylvia."

"Damn it, Jonah, I *hate* when people feel sorry for me. I *hate* sympathy. It's the most useless freaking emotion – don't you think? When people say they feel sympathy for me or empathy for what happened, it makes me feel weak, helpless – like a goddamn little child. I just wish people would feel… awkward around me and not know what to say. I really do. And not have all the 'God bless you' and 'I'll pray for you' Hallmark greeting card phrases down pat – like they're professional grief counsellors or something. I wish people just didn't know what to say or how to act. I wish they'd look away from me because they feel so ashamed and awkward and terrible. Then, I would feel better – like I had some power back or something. Like I wasn't some useless, pathetic, little bastard."

Jonah stops and steers me around by my shoulder to where he can look at my face. I am suddenly aware that there are tears running down my cheeks, and my voice had been faltering.

"Shit, where did this come from?" I wonder out loud. Usually I don't feel much emotion anymore, after having recounted the story so many times to a multitude of therapists. This uninhibited little trickle of feeling that's leaking out surprises me.

"Allergies," I sniffle, looking down. Jonah pulls me in uneasily and wraps me in a tight bear hug. His big grip feels good – relieving and safe.

"I don't know what to say," Jonah says with his chin resting on top of my head. Then he eases his embrace and puts his arm around my shoulders and guides me back into walking again. We hike along, moving forward through the shaded rainforest for a long while, not saying a word. Over a little hill, we come upon an encampment of homeless people – which is not uncommon in Stanley Park. These guys look older and road-weary – probably some Vietnam vets – there are lots of them around here. A few are huddled over a camp-fire and some appear to be passed out, snoring like bears in dirty tattered sleeping bags. A couple of them look up when they hear us coming. Jonah just nods and keeps his eyes on the trail ahead. I feel safe with Jonah. Safer than if I had been with River. River probably would have wanted to stop and talk to them and do some type of intervention. Or get some ethnographic information so he could write a paper about them, or do research on their habitat.

Another half mile down the trail and I have to stop. My feet are raw and bleeding from where the sandal straps have been digging in.

"Crap. I wasn't expecting to go backcountry hiking Jonah. I had no idea it took this long to get to the other side of the park."

"Here," says Jonah as he removes my sandals, then his own shoes and socks as well. He strings the lace from his shoe through the straps of my sandals and swings the two pairs over his shoulders. He reaches out his arm to me and pulls me back up.

"There. Level playing field now. Better?"

"Thanks. Good thing it hasn't rained for a few days." But the ground is still fairly moist beneath our feet and it some-how feels good to have a little thick soil worked in between my toes and onto the open wounds.

An hour later, nearing five o'clock, we finally see the western sun poking through an opening in the trail. The ocean *has* to be through there. Sure enough, as we emerge from the forest, there is a massively large ball of sun hanging low over the Pacific. Just across the narrow roadway is a sandy beach and a little seaside restaurant called The Tea House.

"Come on whitey," Jonah urges as we scamper over the road, down the grassy embankment, and onto the beach. Our dirty feet sink into the still-warm sand.

"We can call a cab in there," Jonah points to The Tea House.

"Sure, if they let us in the door. I heard they have a dress code there. All fancy five-star gourmet stuff. Maybe we should just hitch a ride."

"We won't be eating their food, just using the phone."

We wash our feet in the lapping waves of the ocean, and I sit on the sand to wait while Jonah goes to make the call. He returns in a few minutes.

"Taxi will be here in about forty-five minutes." He sits down beside me.

The sand is still warm and the sky is orange and lavender where the sun is dipping down into the molten Pacific. The air has that fresh salty, fishy smell and seagulls circle and call above us. Jonah is quiet but I can feel his warmth.

There is this person sitting beside me with whom I feel one hundred percent safe and at home with, and I have never felt that way before – with anyone. I turn, touch his face with my hand, and kiss him deeply.

CHAPTER TWENTY
Jonah

It is tense on the cab ride back. For a long time neither one of us says anything. Sylvia just looks out of the side window. I feel her body so close to mine, almost touching, I can feel some warmness coming from her. She's a strange girl, her. She never talked much to me over the last few years she's been coming around to my ma's place. Her eyes watched me a lot though, but she kept her distance, and so did I. Here in the last little while we talked a few times and now she's in love. I wonder what her boyfriend would think of that. I wonder what her parents would think of that.

Remembering back to how it was in my last relationship, it turns me cold. Because I was no good to her – Gina. I was deep into drugs back then and suffering the godforsaken effects from the time spent as a kid in 'the system.' I didn't know how to love, how to trust, how to feel anything besides the anger and the shame. Those are the two worst emotions: anger and shame. They just churn up your guts like a roto-tiller and come exploding out in violence. I didn't know how to deal with it; I took it out on Gina. I beat her bad, and not just once. I hurt our kid too. Gracie Athena. The crying, and crying, and crying, I couldn't handle the sound of it. I shook the baby. And not just once. When we lost Gracie to social services, I never fought it, just figured that was the way things were supposed to go. That I deserved it. And when Gina overdosed, I never even cried. Because the sound of crying just kills me.

Sylvia pats my knee and asks what I am thinking about.

"This can't happen between us." I say.

Sylvia turns her head to me and it looks like she has just finished a hundred-mile marathon. Exhausted. What the hell goes on in a woman's head? Beautiful she is, but young and confused.

"I really like you, Sylvia. But it's not right. And I'm too old for you. You know this."

"What does age have to do with it?"

"It's not the age so much as the experience, Sylvia. I'm from a different place than you. You got to understand that." She looks down and her nose twitches slightly. My brain tells me I am all wrong for her, will do her harm. But nobody can know how lonely I've been, how long I been needing to feel someone looking at me, rather than through me. It's been too many years alone, really alone.

"Jonah, there are more similarities between us than you think."

"There are some, yeah, but that doesn't mean we should get hooked up." I have to tell her this now. She is such a young girl. She still seems like jailbait.

"Jesus, Jonah, you're the one who wanted me to come with you to the Yukon, and then whale hunting up the coast." She is exasperated with me.

I nod my head. I did tease her about those things when I had more fun in me. But things have gotten serious now.

"I'm sorry I led you on that way. It would be nice between you and me – it would be real nice – if it were a different world. But things aren't ever gonna be that way. We have to face the reality. You're hurtin' and I'm hurtin' and two hurtin's together don't make it right – it don't make things better."

"Damn it. I knew I shouldn't have told you about Tommy."

"No Sylvia, I already knew. Well, not all the details, but I read you from the start that you had some things in your past. I got that vibe from you. I know the pain well. I have always liked you, Sylvia. But we are not good for each other."

"What are you running from, Jonah?" She keeps throwing this hard stuff back on me. Ping-pong game shit. What the fuck does she want from me?

"Same can be said about you. What are you running from, Sylvia?"

She is quiet again and looks away out the window. After a few minutes, she turns toward me. She looks hurt and angry.

"Maybe I'm not running away from anything. Maybe I'm running toward something." She wants to keep this going. Dark is coming down onto the city and traffic headlights rush all around us. I see the lights reflected in Sylvia's flashing eyes.

"We are all running toward something, girl. Life or death, and eventually we learn that all roads lead to death."

"And we're just biding our time, right?"

"More or less."

"I can't go on being the person I've been, Jonah. I need to make some changes in my life."

"What, are you having your mid-life crisis in your twenties? And you want a guy to come along and rescue you? Make you feel better about who you are? You said so yourself. You want someone to make you feel more powerful. Well come on then, let's get hooked up and you can feel better about yourself because you date a drunken Indian. Maybe that'll raise you up a notch or two."

She looks hurt and offended now. But I don't care. She needs to hear this stuff. Whatever kind of fairy-tale shit she has in her head has to go. I'm not that guy.

"Jonah I never said — "

"I ain't no wise man, Sylvia. I ain't got all the answers. I ain't got any answers at all. I got nothing to give you but heartache. I'm saying this honestly – for your own good." There's something about her that's asking for too much.

"Jonah, do you ever feel like there's something missing in you? Something that was maybe there once but it's gone now? And I don't mean that in a rude way. Because in me... it seems like something is missing in me too."

I just shake my head. She is pleading now. Trying to get into me – inside the dried-up, hard leather shell. Who is this girl? She's killing me.

"It doesn't matter, Sylvia. None of that shit matters now. This is what the world gave us." Her pretty face looks at me with those sad eyes she probably got when she was younger. She pushes a chunk of hair behind her ear and gnaws on her bottom lip. Something about her makes me feel soft inside and like a little boy again, before the day when they took me away. Before I learned about the bad in the world. Something about her makes me feel like I haven't felt in years, decades. I look down at my dirty grease-pitted hands and remember who I am, where I've been, what was done to me. This girl is looking for something and I can't give it to her.

"I can't be your hero, Sylvia. I'd just let you down."

We are quiet for a while longer until I tell the cab driver to let me off at a pool hall on Granville Street.

"Why are you getting off here?" Sylvia asks, alarmed.

"I need a fuckin' beer," I mumble. Grab my coat, throw down forty dollars for the cab fare to get Sylvia home, and slam the car door. I feel bad that I hurt her, maybe even let her down, but I can't look at her, I have to look away. I feel her soul a lot. I really feel something for her. But she doesn't know who I really am. And all I am is a stranger with a bad story, drifting past, and no one really cares.

As the cab pulls away I hear Sylvia's voice yelling out to my back, "Jonah! We're allowed to go on living you know! It's okay to go on living!"

CHAPTER TWENTY-ONE
Sylvia

After the taxi drops me off in the back alley to my apartment, I stand for a minute scuffing my sandal on the curb. Feeling crushed and despondent. Feeling like a totally useless and powerless fool. What an idiot I am. I let life just walk all over me. A sudden and electrifying impulse jerks me into forward motion to run for the bus that is stopped across the street. It is the bus that will take me to Kitsilano – where River lives. I can't put this off any longer.

Twenty minutes later I'm knocking on River's door. One of his sisters answers. Sunshine, the friendly one. Of course. Damn it.

"Oh hi, Sylvia! Nice to see you. We were just getting dinner ready. Are you hungry? Stay for dinner – nothing fancy, just some curry and rice with sautéed vegetables." Sunshine smiles down sweetly at me.

"Uh no thanks, I already ate a hotdog. I just need to talk to River."

"Sure, come on in."

"Um, actually, can he come out here?" Sunshine looks at me strangely as though I should explain myself. But I can't tell her how I recoil from the thought of entering their happy, glowing vegetarian home. The positive aura is making me cringe and shiver in my fleece jacket. There is too much goodwill emanating from inside and I am about to make it all come crashing down.

River walks around the corner to the foyer. He is his usual upbeat, humming self.

"She wants to talk to you – outside." His sister tells him with her eyebrows raised and an exaggerated shrug.

"Hey Sylvia, what's up? Is something wrong? I should have called you – I was wondering where you were. I just thought I'd give you some space because you were so stressed out lately over exams and everything." River puts a concerned hand on my shoulder as he closes the door behind him. It makes my skin crawl. I can see his two sisters watching us through the kitchen window.

"It's not just that, River." I look up at his face. He's filled with empathy and is wearing that paternalistic look he gets, which makes me feel like I am in a counseling session. But I am not in a counseling session. I am talking to my boyfriend.

"I kissed Jonah."

"What? Who? Jonah? You mean – that guy – you mean Lydie's son Jonah? That Indian guy?" River is understandably incredulous.

"Is that how we refer to him – that Indian guy?" I can feel the sarcasm dripping in the air between us.

"I'm sorry, I meant First Nations person. I'm just shocked.

You kissed him? How – why – how did this happen?"

I sigh. How much can I tell him without telling him too much?

"River, I kissed Jonah today down at the beach in Stanley Park. There is nothing between us. We just kissed."

"Well, what does this mean? Did you have a momentary lapse in consciousness? Are you having some kind of nervous breakdown? Is the notion of an affair some type of sordid escape for you? Should we be looking into therapy for you? Or couples counseling for us both — "

"No, no, no. I don't need therapy. I just need to be alone for a while. I don't want to move in with you River. In fact, I can't see you anymore. I don't want to string you along like I have been. It's not fair for me to treat you that way. So it's over. It has to be."

"Sylvia wait, we need to discuss this, you can't just walk away like that. You need to come in and…and sit down, and be rational and think about this." River goes on and on, jabbering desperately while I stand on the front steps watching his mouth. I watch the way it moves around the words as they form and how every once in a while a little spit flies out involuntarily. The more exasperated he gets, the more this happens. I feel like laughing when I can almost predict each time it will happen.

"Sylvia, are you hearing what I'm saying?" he asks, holding back his hair with his fist as though he is holding himself back from full-out begging.

"No. I'm not into this. There is nothing you can say that will change my mind. It is over River, that's all I can say right now. I apologize for doing it like this. But it's done now. I have to go." I turn and walk down the steps. I pause at the end of the walkway and turn around to look at River. He is absolutely floored.

"Goodbye." That was the word that flew out of my mouth. Not *sorry*, even though I was. But I couldn't say that word again. Too much of my life was spent being sorry.

"Sylvia wait! What about the interview project I asked you about? Boxcar Huey? Remember?"

I can't believe he is thinking about his research project as I walk away from him.

"You'll have to find another homeless drunk to query. Not everything in people's lives is open for academic study and intellectual dissection."

"Wait! You are making a mistake, Sylvia! I'm afraid you will regret this!"

Maybe so. But I turn and walk toward the bus stop.

Instead of going home, I end up at the Roman Coliseum. I'm talking about the Vancouver Public Library, of course. The place is huge, a new-age architect's sanitized and structurally perfect interpretation of the Coliseum in Rome. It is filled with books and quiet, intense people who hole up in the oddest little corners to swim in their literature or do very important research. But the section I make my way to is the lesser traversed area where the staff store all of the archival records, micro-fiches of old newspapers, and the like. There is an elderly lady there behind the desk wearing a frilly ivory-colored blouse and bright, unsightly rouge on her cheeks. She smells a hundred-and-ten-years-old and she seems very happy to see me. Slow day for her, perhaps.

"Hello, how can I help you?" She smiles brightly, her voice crackling with age and old-lady delight at having someone to talk to.

"I want to look up a person who is dead now. But he lived in Vancouver a long time ago and I wanted to see if I could find any record of his life here. I know that he lived here in the 1920s, before the Depression."

"Oh yes, yes dear, I can help you with that. Come with me – do you know his full name? Date of birth? Do you know how to use the micro-fiche?"

Even though I said I do, the old lady walks me through the process and continues to give me advice and bring me old volumes of birth records, census data, and local history books the whole time I'm here – much to my annoyance, and not at all helpful to me. But an hour into my search, I have a hit on the micro-fiche for my Boxcar Huey. There is a late 1920s *Vancouver Sun* newspaper article about a Huey Bonnie Johnson. It has to be him. How many Huey Bonnie Johnsons could there be in Vancouver at that time?

Tragic Fire at Area Home Claims Three Lives

On the night of December the 4th 1929, there was a great house fire at 139 West 22nd Avenue. The house was owned by Mr. Huey Bonnie Johnson, a local salesman. The cause of the blaze has not yet been determined. The home was a total loss and three bodies were later found in the rubble. The deceased have been identified as Mrs. Harriet Johnson, and her two minor children, Huey Junior and Lainey Johnson. Funeral services will be held at the Central Vancouver

Presbyterian Church on Friday at 1:00pm. No public viewing will occur due to the poor state of the bodies. In-kind donations, food and men's clothing (size thirty-six) would be greatly appreciated as Mr. Huey Bonnie Johnson does not have any local relatives to take him in.

Remarkable. Absolutely incredible. River was right in hypothesizing that Boxcar Huey did have some terrible secret buried in his past. It makes me resent River even more. But that still doesn't explain why my mother took in Boxcar Huey. Did she pity him? Could she have known about the house fire so many decades earlier? She never mentioned it, if she did know. She met Huey when she was working as an aide in an old people's home in Medicine Hat. She said she got to talking with him and they realized that her grandmother's maiden name was Johnson, the same Johnsons from Vancouver, where Huey was from. Miriam was the only one Boxcar Huey would deal with. He was belligerent and abusive to all the other aides. And when he got kicked out of the old-age home for having my mom sneak in liquor (and my mom was fired for it), my mother brought him home to stay with us, rather than have him put out on the street again. Now, thinking back, I can recall Huey saying to us kids – in the rare times that he spoke to us at all – that my mother was an *angel* (he always emphasized *angel*) because she was the only one who gave him a home after decades of living on the streets as a hobo. I used to scoff and cringe at the word angel.

But still, why would my mom be drawn to this man? Unlike River, I wouldn't have the gall or the heart to ask her directly. Whatever long-held, undisclosed, enigmatic secret in the relationship that my mother and Boxcar Huey had will go to the grave with them. Some things are better left that way – aren't they?

CHAPTER TWENTY-TWO
The Priest

Paul and a handful of young novices and assistants provide artificial respiration and chest compressions to Father MacAvoy until the paramedics arrive. He is taken by ambulance to the Emergency wing of St. Michael's Hospital in downtown Toronto. An oxygen mask is tethered to his face as he is passed from ambulance to gurney, gurney to table, table to bed. Medical terminology flies from the mouths of the earnest professionals. Voices rush all around him. But he cannot respond.

"Respiratory failure."

"Pupils dilated, fixed."

"Unresponsive to resuscitation – cardiopulmonary arrest."

"Ventricular fibrillation."

"ABG analysis – hypoxia."

"Endotracheal intubation and mechanical ventilation."

"Neurologic deficit – altered level of consciousness."

"Prognosis poor."

"Father MacAvoy, can you hear me?"

Yes, he can hear. But other voices are louder, soon drowning out the electrical sounds of the Intensive Care Unit. Crying, crying children. Screaming. Then…

There is a quietness overhead. The air is still and old, as though it has been untouched for a hundred years. Dusty light shines through the stained glass windows. Father MacAvoy is back at Christ Church Cathedral in Vancouver, where he was reassigned after his three-year stint at the Choutla School in the Yukon. He sits alone in a pew, praying, meditating, contemplating.

Five rows ahead of him is a young man, weeping. The man's white skin has turned red in his anguish and he is hunched over in pain – of the emotional kind. Father MacAvoy leaves his own seat and approaches the young man.

"Is there anything I can do to help you, son? You are in distress."

The man looks up, his blue eyes wracked with torment.

"It's too late for help. I'm done."

"Would you like to join me for a private confessional? You might benefit from some counsel."

The young man slowly rises and follows Father MacAvoy into a small room with wooden chairs. They sit.

"What troubles you, sir?"

"I'm a ruined man. I lost everything. I lost it all three weeks ago – my entire fortune, my business. To the stock market crash on Black Monday. Hell Black Tuesday did me in. It's all been black since then."

"Yes, I've been reading about the fallout from October 29th. How did it happen for you?"

"I'd been persuaded by an investor friend to buy stocks over the last year. I put all my money into them. I lost it all in the crash. Last week I had to close my business, lay off all my staff. I'm bankrupt."

"I'm sorry for your losses. But it is only money. Life will go on. Do you have a family?"

The young man looks up from his stupor to study father MacAvoy's face.

"How will I tell my wife? I have two young children. They go to a good school, they've never wanted for anything in their lives. Soon I will lose the house. The car was repossessed yesterday. My wife still doesn't know. They don't know about any of it, my family. They still think I go to work each day when I leave the house in the morning. But I have no work to go to anymore. So I've been coming here and to other churches, just biding my time."

"To find your salvation?"

"No. To ask for forgiveness."

"But why should you ask for forgiveness when these things that happened were beyond your control. Many have been left bereft and destitute from the stock market crash. I know it must be difficult. But the Lord will provide. You have to have faith."

"Faith is fickle in times like these. I can't have my wife and children sleep in a shelter, or on the street. I can't have my son give up his hockey lessons and my daughter lose her dolls. I can't see them on the streets begging for food. I cannot bear to see my wife without the home that she loves. I can't have them know that their home will be taken away. Faith hasn't given me any answers."

"Then what are you to do?"

This time he looks into the space beyond the priest.

"I will fix it so that they will never know. So that they can sleep peacefully forever in our house on West 22nd."

The man was silent for a long moment.

"Thank you for listening, Father."

"But wait, you have not fulfilled a full confession. I must assign some penance."

"My penance will stalk me to my grave." The man turns his back on the priest as he steps out the door and disappears.

Father MacAvoy was startled by the man's words. The encounter left him deeply troubled. He briefly considered talking to one of his superiors about the incident. But then he reasoned, he might be chastised for letting the man go without allowing him his absolution. Even worse, Father MacAvoy feared what might happen if he broke the seal of the confessional. "*The seal of the confessional is absolute and any confessor who divulges information revealed in confession is subject to deposition and removal from office.*" So say the rules of the Anglican Church of Canada. And Father MacAvoy was not about to find himself in any more potentially perilous situations. He had just avoided catastrophe up north at the Choutla School with that young Indian girl. So he said nothing.

He never saw the man again at the cathedral. But the following week an article in the newspaper caught his eye. It was about a house fire, and a family lost. Wife dead, two children buried in the rubble. Father MacAvoy could hear their screams. He still can. Though he has long since forgotten how they came about, who they were, or why they mattered.

CHAPTER TWENTY-THREE
Miriam

Jesus, the phone is ringing again. I inhale long enough to suck back the smoke all the way into my lungs until I get that sweet buzz that only lasts a second. I remember the times when it lasted a lot longer.

"Damn it Floyd, can't you get that? You know my varicose veins are acting up. It's probably another one of those collection agencies. If it is, I don't live here." The useless ass lumbers up from his chair on the other side of the room and sulks into the kitchen to get the phone on the fifth ring. I can hear him vaguely over the noise of the dishwasher.

"Yeah? Mrs. Lydie Jim? Who? Oh, oh – Sylvia. Hold on."

Floyd hands me the phone with the extra long extension cord.

"Are you sure it's not a bill collector?"

Floyd shrugs and mumbles, "She said she knows Sylvia."

This better not be no freaking joke or fraud scheme.

"Yeah? Who is it?"

"Hello Mrs. Miriam Hardy? My name is Mrs. Lydie Jim and I am a friend of your daughter, Sylvia." This woman on the other end of the phone sounds old and she says "daughter" like "dodder" – half dumb or something.

"Yeah? What do you want from me?"

"I wanted to tell you that your daughter is graduating in a couple weeks. And she too nervous to ask you herself, but I know it would make her happy if you could come to her graduation."

Who the hell is this woman? "What – who? I don't even know who the hell you are."

"My name is Mrs. Lydie Jim. I am from Quiet Lake area of the Yukon. I met your daughter in school at University of British Columbia and we friends now. She told me that she feeling bad because you haven't talked in a long time."

"Did she give you this number?" I demand, trying to uncoil the hopelessly twisted phone cord. I am getting really pissed off now. As if I'm not hounded enough already, now I have some fucking old lady that Sylvia recruited calling me up to hassle me.

"No. Sylvia wouldn't do that. I found the number in her little book. She doesn't want to bother you. But she still loves you Mrs. Hardy. And she misses you."

I am floored. Who is this stranger calling me up out of the blue and talking about my kid? What kind of person does that?

"What the hell do you know about it?"

"I know it's hard when you lose a child Mrs. Hardy. Or when they get taken away. Ain't nothing anybody can say that matters or helps or that you can understand after you lose a child. I know it's real hard grief because I been there myself. I been taken away from Quiet Lake and then I had my babies taken away. And it made me real mad for a while too. Real mad and sad and I didn't know what to do or who to hate 'cause of it. But then I remember how much I love my babies, even the little time we had together. And how I love them now when they come back to me, even though they be changed by the people that took them."

"Yeah, well at least you got yours back. My baby ended up being a pile of bones in some dusty cow patty up in the goddamn Badlands. And only a few bones were ever found. So the rest of my baby is scattered around on the wind. And they never caught the bastard that did it." This stuff just blurts out of me from some very angry place.

"I lost my first baby in a mystery too. She fall somehow out of a boat and she drownded in the river. Gracie. My only girl child. Nobody knew how or why she fall over, but she did. Some tried to save her, but it too late. Then I had my two boys, and every day I look at them and thank the Creator for giving me these to love."

"That's nice. Why did you call me?"

"I call you to tell you that you need to know you still have two daughters. You still have those girls that love you and you lost one child but that not Sylvia's fault. I see her still a little girl, wanting mummy to love her. But mummy so sad. Mummy needs to know that she only lost one baby that day, not three."

"I can't deal with this crap. You don't know shit about me." I motion aggressively to Floyd – who has been watching me from the kitchen – to hang up the phone. He presses the receiver button and the line goes dead.

"Who was that?" he asks.

"Some damn old lady that Sylvia knows."

Floyd asks what she wanted, but I ignore him – he doesn't really care anyway – and light up another cigarette. *Deep breath and...there...relaxation.* I feel really tired now. Really, really, tired. I get up off my chair to pass the receiver back through into the kitchen and as I do this, I catch an image in the mirror on the living room wall. There is some stranger there grimacing back at me. Some rundown, aged woman with dark bags under her droopy eyes and lines creased around her tight, thin lips. She looks really haggard and half-way to her grave. I reach up a hand and touch the face. Sure enough, I feel the coldness of my fingers on my cheek so I know that it's mine.

I don't need this emotional bullshit drama in my life. I already have enough to worry about. I sit back down in the worn reclining chair. I don't hate Sylvia. It's just hard for me to think of her, is all. When I think of her it brings back all the memories from that day in Calgary and all the stuff after it. Everything changed that day.

Before Tommy was taken, I was a good mom. I really tried to be. I taught both my girls how to sew and quilt and took them to piano lessons once a week. We used to go for picnics out along the rest areas on the highway, and go swimming in the reservoir in the summertime. Even though I didn't get very far in school myself, I used to help the girls with their homework. I tried to do my best for them – it was hard, I was so young and a single mother for a while until

Floyd came along and he never was much help with the kids anyway. Just like Pierre. I tried real hard to make up for picking shitty fathers. But it never was enough. Sylvia went and called the social services on me when she was about fourteen years old. She put in an anonymous call pretending she was a nosy neighbor saying that I drank too much and neglected my kids. I know it was her because the social services case worker told me they figured it out after talking to Sylvia's guidance counselors at school. They made us all go to family counseling but that fell by the wayside after a while.

I tried my best with those two girls. Especially Sylvia because she was always pushing my buttons and challenging me. The oldest daughter. I really tried hard to make sure they had a fun time when they were little. Helped them much as I could with their projects and their reading. And Tommy with his words. He was just learning to put things together. He was an adorable little boy – everybody thought so. He was a little chunker with beautiful sparkling eyes, mesmerizingly cute. I kept his hair buzzed real short, so he never lost that baby look about him. He smiled and grinned at everyone he saw and he was just like this ray of sunshine in our lives. He really was.

I remember the smell of him. I used to tell him, "Tommy, mmmm…you smell like a macaroni!" And he'd laugh and giggle.

He was a little bit behind in his development, and that cleft palate thing he was born with affected his speech. He wasn't really speaking words when he was two years old, and certainly not sentences. But looking back, I see now that it was a good thing. He just smiled and laughed and didn't ever get the chance to grow into a sassy, foul-mouthed thing who talked back to me like his older sisters did. No, when I think of him, he is still the sweet little angel who would nuzzle his head into my belly and pat-pat my belly with his chubby little hand.

"Me - in - dere?" he would always ask and I would tell him, "Yes, you come from in there, from mommy's belly."

I remember the day I went to see him after he was found. Or, what was left of him. His remains were kept in a small box at the RCMP crime lab up in Edmonton. The detectives gave me permission to go and view the bones, since that's all there was left of my baby. It was one of those painfully cold prairie winter days in late February when I drove up there. I remember the way the car tires crunched and cracked on the side streets so early in the morning when I left the house, and even with the heat blasting, my breath was still visible in the car for miles up the highway. I hadn't warmed up the old Cadillac properly because I wanted to be gone before the girls woke for school so they wouldn't ask where I was going. My hands were aching from clutching the freezing steering wheel. It was so cold it made my fingers feel like they were on fire through my thin leather gloves.

At the RCMP station, I turned down an offer of hot coffee in a Styrofoam cup from the lead detective on the case. I couldn't eat or drink anything that morning or all that day afterward. I guess those cops are desensitized about that sort of thing. Then they took me into a room – a lab-type room full of long metal tables and industrial refrigerators and shelving full of labelled containers and boxes. That is not a place where little children should be. They said the room was an evidence preservation room. There on the middle table, laid-out in preparation for me, was a small crate about the size of a clothing gift-box from Sears. Inside was my Tommy.

I saw his little hand bones, those tiny fingers, a small piece of his jawbone, the distorted little maxilla and part of his miniature skull. I looked for a long time. Then I asked if I could touch them. My hands still ached from the cold, but now they ached for my Tommy, to feel him. The detective told me no, the remains needed to be properly preserved as evidence since it was still an open case, so I could only look.

"It's weird isn't it? How we make these little creatures and usually we die before them so we should never get to see this part of them. And here I am standing, looking down at my baby's bones. All the time I held him in my arms alive, I would never have gotten to see this part of him. And now here I am, looking at my baby's empty white bones. Empty of him. Because the softness of him is gone from here, forever."

The detective nodded and put his hand on my shoulder and told me how sorry he was. Then he put the lid on the box and Tommy disappeared again.

He used to sing in his crib. I would lie in bed for hours some-times in the morning, just listening to him sing alone in his crib. No real words, but he could almost carry a tune. His songs were unrecognizable – but they were songs. His voice so soft and sweet, silly, laughing and musical. Even after the reconstructive surgery, through that scarred disfigured little mouth, his song would come through. I remember the sound of him singing to himself alone in his crib.

And I still remember how he used to smell. I'd say, "Yummy! You smell like cheese and macaroni!" And I'd pretend to eat his wiggly-piggy toes. And he'd laugh and laugh and hug my belly and I'd feel his chubby little hand on my back, going pat-pat-pat, pat-pat-pat.

CHAPTER TWENTY-FOUR
Lydie

Sylvia is on her way over. She said she was bringing her knitting bag so I know that means she wants to have a quiet day inside. We do knitting together – tuques, scarves, mittens – and give them all away. We do this about once a month when Sylvia is in a quiet mood and don't feel like talking much. But she don't mind if I talk. Fact, I think she likes to have her quiet times so I can talk and talk and maybe she thinks along in her head and figures things out. That's what I try to do with these youngsters – tell them stories about the old days and teach them lessons. That way maybe they learn something that ain't showing up in the textbooks at school.

Sylvia girl comes to my door with her knitting bag and she looks really tired and down. I put on some fresh tea for us and get us all arranged on the chesterfield. Sylvia is kind to me, she always is, but she in her own world today. I chit-chat and tell her how my final exams went and how excited I am

CHAPTER TWENTY-FIVE
The Priest

"Will he survive?" Paul asks with great concern. "He is very old."

"Yes, he is, and the prognosis is poor. He has many complications – severe neurological injury, pulmonary and cerebral edema, multiple organ system failure. We are doing everything we can but I'm afraid he is essentially in a vegetative state. He is comatose."

"Is there any chance that he will come out of it?"

"There is always a chance. But in his case, it's not likely. His systems are all shutting down. The machines are keeping him alive. He is showing signs of seizure activity with frequent full-body spasms, fluttering eyelids, knee jerks."

"Yes, I have seen these things. Is that not proof that he might wake up?"

"I'm sorry, I know that you want him to survive. But at this point I would advise you to contact his next of kin."

"We are his family, doctor. But I will take your words to my superiors."

Father MacAvoy could hear this conversation. It made his heart ache for Paul. Father MacAvoy was helpless, but Paul was more helpless. There is nothing worse than that feeling of helplessness.

It was nearly a decade after he left Choutla School and after the house fire tragedy in Vancouver when Father MacAvoy received a letter from Lydie. It was scribbled in pencil on lined yellow paper, addressed to him personally via the Christ Church Cathedral in Vancouver. Lydie must have done some letter writing and researching to find him there. Her letter was a plea.

June 6, 1939
Dear Father MacAvoy,
Hello kind Father. It has been many years since you seen
me but I am all growed up now and married. My husband
Samuel Jim and I just found out that we are going to have
a baby! But that is not why I am writing you from the
Yukon.

I read in the newspaper out of Whitehorse today that
President Roosevelt said that the St. Louis ship was not
allowed to come to shore in the USA with all them Jewish
refugees on board. The paper said that ship is now headed
to Canada to try to land so that the Jews could get off here
and live in peace and not have to worry about going to
concentration camps like Hitler is making all the other Jews
do. But the folks are saying that Prime Minister Mackenzie

*King won't let them come ashore here in Canada neither
since he says that them Jews are not a Canadian problem.*

*Father MacAvoy, I didn't know who else to turn to!
Those poor Jews can't go back to Germany or Europe! That
Hitler has been taking away all their rights, citizenship,
houses, and businesses. I been reading about this stuff in the
newspapers and listening on the radio. Father MacAvoy, as
a priest, isn't there something that you can do? Can't you
pick up your telephone and ring Mr. Mackenzie King and
tell him to let those Jewish people come to Canada?*

*I wrote a letter to the Prime Minister too, but I don't
expect him to listen to an Indian girl from way up in the
Yukon. But he would listen to you Father MacAvoy. Being a
man of God, you would be able to make him listen and do
the right thing.*

*Think of all them Jews on the boat. Maybe you don't
feel too much sympathy for the Jews because you are
Anglican, but they're people just like you and me. And think
of the little Jews – the children – they so innocent, they ain't
done nothing wrong. Please find a way to help them Father
MacAvoy.*

Sincerely,
Mrs. Lydie Jim

Father MacAvoy quietly folded the letter up and placed it
back into its envelope. Reading the letter made him feel very
tired and heavy. He needed to lie down for a spell. Three hours
later, when he awoke, he sat down at his desk with his writing
supplies. The least he could do was to give her a reply.

June 20, 1939
My Dearest Lydie,
I'm afraid your letter has reached me too late. The St. Louis was denied entry into Canada and with provisions on board dwindling drastically low, the ocean liner had no choice but to return to Europe. Fear not though. Countries such as France, Belgium, and Holland have agreed to take in some of the Jewish refugees – surely they will be safe in those countries from the reach of the Nazi Party.

In any case, there is not much a priest in my position could have done. As a Holy man, I try to stay out of the secular realm of politics as much as possible. It simply isn't the place for a priest to interfere. God will take care of everyone and sort things out in the end. It doesn't take a lowly human being like you or me to make the changes that the world needs.

Nonetheless, it was very good to hear from you.

Sincerely,
Father MacAvoy

Decades would pass before the priest learned of the fate of the passengers of the *St. Louis*. In 1976 he watched a new motion picture titled *Voyage of the Damned* – based on the real life story of the Jewish refugees aboard the *St. Louis*. In the end, he learned that many of the passengers who had found refuge in places such as France and Belgium fell prey to the Nazi killing machine when the Germans invaded those countries. Most of the people aboard the ship eventually died in concentration camps.

It was with this grim fact in mind that Father MacAvoy and some fellow Anglican priests made a trip to Auschwitz-Birkenau in southern Poland during a European vacation in 1984. They took a guided tour of the former Nazi concentration camp. At the entrance the guide told them they were about to encounter the largest extermination site in Nazi-occupied Europe.

They proceeded through the gates where the Jewish prisoners would have entered into slave labor not so many decades ago. Overhead, were the iron words *Arbeit Macht Frei*. Their guide translated for them. "Work Will Make You Free." They walked into the compound to view the prisoner administration building, the prisoner kitchen, the tree out front where Jews were tied and punished with whippings and attack dogs for merely stealing bread. There was a small, narrow, and dark structure at one edge of a plaza-like square. "This is where the Rapportfuhrer commanded the roll call," the guide explained. "This is one of the locations where the 'selections' were made. Separating out the weaker and sending them to their deaths, while the ones who still remained strong were preserved for the benefit of their labor."

In all his travels, never before had the priest taken a tour where the guide's face was so hardened and pained. The guide never once smiled, nor would it have been appropriate.

"It is such a pity," one of the priests muttered, "that this place has such a marred history. It is so beautiful now with the sun shining through the leafy trees."

The guide had overheard him.

"In fact, those trees were much smaller in the early 1940s. But they were here and they witnessed all the atrocities, though only their souls speak of it now, their beauty does not reveal their past."

Father MacAvoy considered the guide's words as he ran his hand over the bark of one of the large trees. Next, they toured the empty barracks, the camp hospital where the ill were not treated but experimented on and then sent to their death in the gas chambers. There was a camp "jail." *How odd,* thought Father MacAvoy, *for there to be a jail in the middle of a concentration death camp.* Between Blocks No. 11 and No. 12, was the Death Wall at the end of the long, narrow courtyard. Thousands had been lined up there and shot in the head by SS guards. It was a memorial now.

Unimaginable tortures and deaths were orchestrated in Blocks 11 and 12. The brutal science experiments, the forced sterilizations, starvation, suffocation, gassings and deaths in three-foot-square, stand-up detainment cells. The horror of it all was worse than the priest had ever imagined. *So many innocent souls lost, such utter suffering,* he thought to himself.

Then they entered the gas chamber at the Krematorium I. It was like a long basement structure, below ground, no windows, very old reinforced concrete. So many marks and scuffs on the solemn walls. *Are they left from the people?* Father MacAvoy wondered. And there is the rectangular hole in the ceiling through which the deadly gas crystals were poured by SS guards wearing ghostly gas masks. Next to the death room, was the Krematorium room. Large brick ovens with half-round metal doors featured rail carts to slide the bodies into the flames. *How can it be that so many innocent people were killed here?* the priest asked himself. *Did no one take pity?* The tour guide and the others moved on, but the priest lingered in the doorway between the death room and the crematorium.

It was so quiet, still.

Then the priest saw a vision. It started in the gas chamber. A young woman holding an infant to her chest. The woman was naked and he could see that her skin was brown, dark brown like a Native's skin. She did not look at him – she could not see him – but when he saw her face, he could see that she was clearly an Indian woman, like the kind in Canada. A white-faced SS guard appeared and violently shoved her toward the crematorium room. She must have survived the gassing, as did her child. She was beaten with the butt of the guard's gun to force her to climb into the little train cart on rails that led to the oven. He made her lie down, the baby still whimpering in her arms. The priest stood looking over her in the cart, paralyzed – he could not speak. The woman's face contorted with terror, grief, anguish, and the likes of which he had never seen before. But that was not true; he had seen it before. The SS guard lurched the little train coffin forward into the oven and slammed the metal door shut with a horrific groan of ancient steel.

"Father MacAvoy?" One of the senior priests interrupted the vision, effectively dissipating it and returning the priest to the otherwise empty room.

"It is not difficult to be overtaken by the cruelty of it all," the senior priest said softly. "You've gone right pale – have you seen a ghost?"

"Many. I've seen many ghosts," Father MacAvoy responded, trembling.

"So much death. So many innocents," the senior priest

said as he waved his arm around the impenetrable concrete room. "And why? Because they were different. Because they did not meet the Euro-centric ideals of blonde hair and blue eyes. The greater tragedy, I'm afraid, is that we allowed this to happen. Yes, *we*. That we were complacent, complicit in all of this."

What is my role in all of this genocide? Father MacAvoy wondered.

He still wonders now, as he lies comatose in a bed at St. Michael's Hospital in downtown Toronto.

Should I have used my voice?

CHAPTER TWENTY-SIX
Sylvia

Anything can change in an instant. Anything can change with the blink of an eye, the flick of a switch, the signing of a signature, or the turning of a wheel. One step in this direction will take you somewhere. One step in that direction will take you somewhere entirely different. Any arbitrary decision you make will change your life. You'll just never know how.

Lydie wants me to be patient and take one decision at a time. She wants me to see that no matter what choices are made, something good *and* bad can come of it. Lydie has been a good friend to me. I know that all the time we have spent together over the last couple of years has impacted me and changed me for the better. I'm still messed up, of course. But I'm lucky to have her in my life.

We spent the better part of the day knitting and when I came home, I was even focused enough to work on my green dress for an hour or two. I guess now that school is done,

I have entered into a very productive mode. My hands are working sinuously and functionally. The itch to do something mindless and physical is very strong.

Mui and I are planning a night out on the town with the girls tonight. It has been a long time coming. And I am looking forward to it very much. I really need to get down, do some dancing, act like a fool with no cares, and get really drunk.

Eight o'clock and we are all gathered at our apartment, getting dressed in our barhopping outfits, downing Margaritas, and letting off steam by gossiping wildly. All seven of us are hooting it up now that we are done exams. In a daring move, because I am feeling reckless and naughty, I am wearing this nifty sleeveless vest I made. It is faux leather – black – tight and sluttish. It pushes my small breasts together in some semblance of cleavage and it feels empowering. I also have on a hiked-up plaid "school-girl" mini-skirt, a pair of fishnets, and lace-up stiletto boots I borrowed from Mui. She can be vampy too when she wants to be.

At 10:00 we are already buzzing and heading out the door into the cool night for some downtown festivities. We take the rowdy bus full of young people heading the same direction down to Gastown and start hopping the pubs there. The first one is a neat little upstairs joint that features live Reggae and Ska. We load up on drinks at the bar and claim a table. I am itching to dance, so I grab Mui and march onto the floor and really let loose. We do this for about five songs until we are breathless, then we down our drinks, grab the gals and head for another pub. This time we opt for an Irish joint that plays hard-core Celtic fiddle and East Coast music. I love that stuff so I grab another beer, drink half of it very fast, and hit the dance floor with people I don't even know. We whoop and we holler and we jump and bang our feet to the Celtic beat of the snare drums and we shake our hands in the air and clap and sing until our voices are raspy.

It feels good just to let it all go and not care what happens next.

At one point Mui and Julie approach me.

"Pace yourself, Sylvia. We don't want to have to carry you home."

"Hey, I'm having a good time. Let me be!" Mui and Julie fade off into the crowd again.

After an hour or so, I meet this group of college guys and they are generously buying me shots. Just to prove what a cool cat I am, I do enough shots to keep up with them. By now my head is swimming so when Meadow – one of River's sisters – approaches me I don't even recognize her at first.

"Sylvia, hey, what's up?" she says. She's smiling so I bet she doesn't know yet about the break-up with River.

I say hi, then – out of the blue – a fit of laughter takes over me and I can't control myself. "That is the fucking funniest name I have ever heard! Meadow!" I crack myself up and the guys buying me shots are howling too and egging me on.

"Are you okay, Sylvia? River mentioned a while ago that you were kind of acting strange." Meadow moves closer to me in an apparent act of concern.

"Strange? You want to know what's strange? Your sister's name! Sunshine!" I screech as I see Sunshine come up behind Meadow. Once again my posse is howling, and Meadow looks absolutely bewildered.

"What is strange is your behavior, Sylvia Hardy," Sunshine

says with not a ray of sunshine. Obviously, River let her in on the news.

"What is strange is your behavior and going around hurting my brother and not even explaining why. What have you got to say about that?" Sunshine stares me down with contempt and steel in her eyes. Sunshine is the morally superior sister. Then River steps up next to me.

"Hey, let's cool it down girls. Sylvia, you look like you've had way too much to drink. Why don't you come with me?"

"How did you know where I was? Have you been following me?" I'm shouting into River's face.

"No, but I did call and talk to Mui earlier today and she mentioned you would be down in this area of Gastown. So I thought I'd watch out for you."

River's statement nearly sends me over the edge. I can't believe he would have to gall to call Mui to check on me, and even worse, I can't believe Mui didn't tell me. And she told River *where* I would be going! I feel so completely violated and betrayed.

"You jerk. Leave me alone. I don't need someone 'watching out' for me and stalking me around."

"Cool down, Sylvia. Let's not do this here. I really think you should come home with me – I'm here because I care about you," River says paternalistically, flanked by his army of righteous sisters.

"Come on, Sylvia. You need to get out of this bar. You are crossing the line," Sunshine adds.

"Back off!" I warn them.

River takes a step forward and takes hold of my arm. "Sylvia, you need help. I'm here to help you."

talking to you! Hey! HEY! WHY CAN'T I TOUCH YOUR FUCKING HAIR?!"

I scream at them with all that is left in me and collapse to the ground, multicolored lights twinkling in my eyes as I go and a strange ringing sound in my ears. Everything goes black.

Some time later Jonah is at my side.

"Sylvia, Sylvia, wake up woman."

I blink myself awake. The beginning reds and oranges of early dawn are creeping into the cool night sky between the downtown buildings.

"What time is it?" I ask, still feeling drunk, but much more sick and serious now. "How did you find me?"

"It's almost five, and you're a hard girl to track down. I been riding around for hours looking for you. Let's get you the hell out of here. What were you doing down here anyway? Trying to turn some tricks?"

I look down at the bare feet covered only slightly by tattered fish-net stockings, now ripped and running; the tight little plaid skirt riding up my thighs; and the faux leather vest, which is now somewhat deformed from the rain and my perspiration.

"I got drunk."

"Come on then, let's get you home," Jonah says as he pulls me up from one of those old smelly Hudson's Bay blankets.

"Where the hell did you steal this from?" Jonah asks. He looks sort of amused.

"I...I have no idea. Maybe those guys across the street..." My words trail off as the vomit lurches up from my stomach. It is projectile and leaves me heaving. More follows.

Jonah holds my head and hair and murmurs small words of comfort. My breath is shallow between spells of vomiting. My skin is cold and clammy – pale bluish when I glance down at my hands on the concrete.

"Jesus, Sylvia, I think you got alcohol poisoning. You over-did it, girl. I better take you to a hospital – you can die from that shit."

I don't remember much of what happened next – only that they pumped my stomach, and that is not an experience that I would ever like to revisit. Jonah waited by my side while I slowly recovered some of my faculties and intestinal functioning. A gentle gray-haired nurse fitted an oxygen mask on me to help with the breathing and hooked some intravenous fluids into me. The doctor came in and told me he wasn't going to release me just yet – I could have died after all – he was going to admit me to the hospital for monitoring.

How long would I be in? I wanted to know. He said twenty-four hours ought to be enough to make sure my stomach had settled down. Jonah had to bee at work by eight o'clock that morning so he left a half-hour before. He said he would tell Lydie and have her come down and sit with me. But since she is not related to me, she won't be allowed in until visiting hours – and that's not until four in the afternoon.

So here I am, drifting in and out of a nauseous sleep in a crisp white hospital bed. They put me in a communal room on the adult ward, but my bed is the only occupied one out of the four. I sleep it off for most of the morning. An orderly brings me lunch on a tray but I can barely even look at it, let alone put some in my mouth. My mind is swimming with the agonizing memories of the previous night, interrupted only by the occasional nurse who comes in to check my vitals.

The nurses on this shift are all young, maybe even the same age as me or younger. They are not like the matronly, sympathetic nurse who held my hair as I puked into a metal kidney dish in the emergency room. No, these young things have an attitude of superiority and aloofness emanating from their pores. They walk in silently but curtly, without even greeting me, and rush over to grab at the I.V. tubes. I can see by their eyes that they don't think of me as an equal; instead, they either dismiss me or glance over me from top to bottom, judging every bruise and mud stain. The information must be printed in block letters on my chart – HANDLE WITH CARE: THIS ONE IS MENTAL! – because all the young nurses who flit in treat me the same way. They are cold and reserved, as though they themselves had never gone out and had one too many.

By the time Lydie arrives (at 4:00 pm on the dot) my hands are clammy from clenching the covers. I have been going over every humiliating thing that has ever happened to me in my life, and this one ranks somewhere up near the very top.

"Oh Sylvia! You okay, girl?!" Lydie cries as she swoops down to gather me in a hug.

"Never better," I croak.

"You don't have to talk – you just lay there and get better. I'll do the talking."

True to her word, Lydie sat by my side for the entire three-hour visiting period and told me every story she could recall from growing up in the Yukon. She even made me chuckle a few times. She washed my face and neck.

"These stupid nurses don't do no helping or washing like they used to. Nowadays, you got to do everything yourself in these hospitals," Lydie griped.

And before she left, she held my hand and fed me some soup.

Jonah came to collect me in the early morning the next day. The doctor finally released me after a long lecture about the risks of binge drinking to vulnerable young women like myself.

Jonah drove me to my apartment on the back of his motorcycle, with my head lolling and flopping around on his shoulder. He helped me inside and down the stairs and then sat down at the kitchen table while I made coffee. I called Mui at her girlfriend's house and told her I was okay. She was only a little pissed-off at me for taking off and for not calling her sooner. Oh, and for the missing boots that I had ditched in some alley somewhere. I told her I'd pay her back later. And that I was really, really sorry. What else could I say?

"Want some toast or something?" I ask Jonah.

"You're the hung-over one. I don't need any toast."

"You telling me you never get totally wasted?"

"No. Liquor doesn't have that affect on me," he says.

"But I thought you were an alcoholic? At least, that's what Lydie always said about you."

"Like I said, I never get wasted. Why is this your business anyway?"

"It's not. Whatever. I'm a jerk."

"Yeah, well we're all jerks at one time or another. Don't beat yourself up over it. I have to head to work. You should shower – you don't smell too good. You okay now?"

Once again, "Never better. Shower sounds like a fine idea, actually. Thanks for the rescue and ride home."

"You should never drink alone," Jonah says.

"I wasn't. I was at a bar with friends. I left them there and took off."

"Then you should never go off by yourself when you are drinking. Alcohol does weird things to the mind when you're all alone. It feels helpful at first, maybe. But then there ain't no way out, it sucks you right in – once you're down, you're all alone in a deep pit."

"Gee, thanks for the advice, Dad."

"Sometimes I wish to hell I was your father, Sylvia. I'd kick your goddamn stubborn ass."

"Violence always helps the situation."

"You know what I mean. I have to go. I'm gonna be late for work."

"Why are you so afraid of me, Jonah?" I'm talking to his back as he heads up the stairway to the door. What have I got to lose now? He's seen me at my absolute worse. I hate the feeling of him walking away.

"I'm afraid of nothing but myself, Sylvia. Same as you. Two wrongs don't make a right. I told you that before."

"Maybe we won't always be wrong," I yell, just as he starts his raging motorcycle engine.

"Please don't leave me, Jonah – I need you!" But he couldn't have heard. He was already gone.

An hour later finds me in the shower, washing all the makeup and filth from my body, crying out the events of my life.

CHAPTER TWENTY-SEVEN
Jonah

All day today and yesterday at the shop, I couldn't shake the sight of her. Laying there on the street corner. Dark purple hair all around her head. Reaching up for me. Only the second time in my life someone ever reached up for me, and on the first time I couldn't handle it. That damn Sylvia's got me frazzled. But just thinking about her still makes me smile.

On my lunch break, I look her number up in the phone book. Turns out I can't let this go after all.

But she doesn't answer. Probably sleeping it off. I leave her a message: "Sylvia, it's me, Jonah. Hope I wasn't too hard on you when I dropped you off. Listen, it'd be good if we could go somewhere to talk. I'll pick you up after work a little after four today. Dress warm, we'll go on my bike."

I didn't give her the option of bailing out. Just figured we should get away for a bit and talk sober. I didn't even go with the guys for a beer today at lunch. So she can't say she smells alcohol on my breath. The smell of it might push her over the edge anyway. I remember how it goes when you're young and liquor is new.

Used to be that I could be with a woman and not feel much. It was that way for a long time. With Sylvia, it feels completely different. She's a whole different breed. Even when she's falling down drunk, there's something about her…I don't see her like those other women at the bars. There's something about her that is childlike – she's a grown woman, sure, but something about her pulls at my heart like when I look into the eyes of a child. But maybe that's not even the right way to describe it. When I look into her eyes, something of her soul…it's almost like looking at myself when I was a kid. A kid I had forgotten about a long, long time ago. When I'm with Sylvia, I feel this thing, this feeling that I thought I lost forever, many years ago.

Four fifteen, after a quick shower and clothes change, I'm knocking on the door to her basement apartment. She answers at the fifth knock.

"Well, well, my knight in shining armor has returned," she says in that sarcastic voice.

"Fuck off! I'll leave."

"No!" She grabs my jacket sleeve, laughing. "I was just kidding! You look nice." She pulls me around to face her. She looks really pretty in a green dress with some delicate stitching, kind-of hippy-ish with an old sweater on top and some suede boots.

"Nice dress on you."

"Thanks. I made it. Just finished it today. Sewing is a good thing to do when you're hung over, recovering from alcohol poisoning. But I finished it."

"You look real fine in it."

"Fine huh? Is this a date, with all the compliments or… what's the deal?"

"I just thought you might want to get away for a bit – help you get over your mental breakdown."

Sylvia throws her head back in laughter.

"What a head case you must think I am."

"Forget about it. You learned your lesson. Hopefully. Come on."

"Where are we going? You haven't told me? Up to the Yukon? Should I have packed an overnight bag?" She grins.

"No. Just over to Gibsons. I thought it would be nice to get out of the Vancouver fog and pollution. And Gibsons is real close by ferry."

"Well alright. I've never been to those rugged parts before, but okay. You're the captain on this one."

Sylvia slides easily onto the seat behind me and put her arms around my middle. The feel of her there was incredible. But I can't trust in her, in this feeling. It's all too fleeting and thin. Like a guitar string – ready to snap at any moment and sting me. It never lasts; it's never real. I think briefly of the woman Sylvia caught me in bed with. The look on Sylvia's face, the hurt in her eyes.

I drive over to the terminal dock at Horseshoe Bay, pay the fee, and maneuver my bike onto the ferry. It's less than an hour's ride to Gibsons just across Howe Sound, but we walked up to the top deck to look around.

"Beautiful. Invigorating." Sylvia says in an almost musical voice as the salty breeze and the boat's momentum nearly push us into one another.

"Yeah. Amazing mountain range views from here. Gibsons is just up the way there – a neat little place. I think you'll like it. Lots of artsy, crafty people there," I tell her.

She turns her gaze slowly to my face and smiles a smile like we are old friends. She slips her little white hand through my arm and huddles tight to me. "Cold," she says shivering up to me. My breath almost stops.

Once we dock and exit the Langdale Ferry Terminal, I ride us along the highway a little ways into the town site up on the hill overlooking Howe Sound. I drive up a few main streets of Gibsons to give Sylvia an idea of the place. She seems pleased – pointing at things and giving me the thumbs-up sign, slapping my knee. Near the end of Molly's Lane Market is a little restaurant that serves good steaks and fresh fish. I pull up my bike in front.

"Hungry? Got your appetite back? They got good grub here."

"It's quaint. This whole town is really phenomenal. It looks almost like a movie set."

We walk inside the darkened restaurant and are seated at a table by the window, with candles burning in empty wineglasses and all that ambience crap. We both order the fresh-caught halibut with baked potatoes and summer vegetables on the side. For dessert it's blueberry pie for me and peach cobbler on Sylvia's side of the table. The food is so good that we are quiet most of the time, just enjoying the taste and the evening sunlight. But every time I look up, I catch Sylvia smiling at me. Once or twice she even winked at me. The little tart.

After dinner, Sylvia pulls me down the sidewalk to look in some of the boutiques that have caught her eye. She has to look in all of the artisan and antique shops, at every little polished rock and candleholder. Then she spends nearly a half hour in a boutique, trying on handmade clothes and asking me which one I like best on her. I sit on a bench outside smoking and she twirls out every five minutes wearing another colorful number. She finally settles on a long earth-toned skirt that I tell her will fit right into her hippy wardrobe. She laughs at this statement.

Then down to the Gibsons wharf, Sylvia marvelling at the picturesque coastline, and I point out the majestic old growth cedars, maple and hemlock. We sit in the gazebo watching the clouds roll off the mountains and the sun dip low, low in the sky, leaving color washes of red, orange and something like purple.

This quiet between us is peaceful, but I do begin to wonder what she is thinking.

"How did your roommate take your little adventure?" I ask.

"Mui? She had a small tantrum, which is only fair – I deserved to be shit on. She's emotional that way. Then she cooked me noodles. She's like that. She has her quirks."

"I had a peculiar roommate once myself. When I was in college. He was this Indian guy – real Indian, like from India, you know? Yeah? Studying geophysics or some darn science thing and I can't even remember the guy's name but I remember that every frigging time he got out of the shower, I had to

are too many barriers. Too many walls between us." Sylvia gets up and walks out the door. But I can't just let her go.

I run after her and catch her by the arm around the corner of the building, and in some uninhibited desperation, almost knock her into the stone wall. She gasps and looks at me as though she is scared or angry – or both. I am surprised at my own panic.

"You going to throw a punch or something?" I tease in a weak response to the look on her face and her momentary silence.

"Jonah, you practically threw me against the wall!"

"I'm sorry Sylvia. I didn't mean for that to happen." *But that is what I am afraid of – I know it will happen, I know I will hurt her.* "It just freaked me out when you got up and left like that. You are making me crazy."

In one quick motion Sylvia shoots her hand up and yanks – hard – at my hair.

"There. Now we're even, *he-man*. You have met your match." Sylvia has laughter in her eyes.

She makes me laugh. She has a way of doing that.

"Girl, I wish you didn't have such a hold on me. Lately I can't get you out of my thoughts."

She shakes her head lightly and looks past my shoulder, and then up to meet my eyes again. My hand finds its way to her face. The feel of her is warm in the rain-cooled air. I bring her face into my chest and just hold her there. We stand that way for a long time. Neither of us talking, just soaking in the sensation of each other. Just like we'd been lovers forever.

In the end, we get a room for the night.

In our room I ask her, "You sure you want to go there with me? I'm nearly forty you know."

"I'm no spring lamb, Jonah. I feel forty every day. Heck, some days I feel like I'm fifty," she says, shaking her head as if to shed something from the past.

But I know what she means. I have been lonely too long. And it ages you more than you can tell. All those other women meant nothing, just like I meant nothing to them. I was so lost in the past. So lost to the world, lost to me. Sylvia can understand that about me.

And later, after we're done and lying close together with her head nestled on my chest, she says, "There is something that you and I have together, Jonah. Please don't deny it. There's something really profound that we share."

"I'm not denying it," I tell her gently. "And now we'll always have Gibsons."

She pushes back her hair. But her eyes are in some faraway land. It's time to start coming clean with her. I owe that to her.

"Sylvia, I have to go away for a while. And you won't see me for a long time. Soon, I have to be leaving Vancouver. It's the only way I can deal with my stuff. And I don't know what the outcome will be. But I have to at least try."

CHAPTER TWENTY-EIGHT
Lydie

My baby boy I hold tight in my arms. Four days 'till graduation ceremony, but he has to leave before then. The treatment
center won't delay its program for no one. If you want to get
sober, they say, you come now.

Jonah is my baby. He's all growed up but he was the last
born of my babies so it's okay for me to hold him in my arms
and cry because he's going away. But I know it will be good
for him. He tried before in a center down here in Vancouver
to get better but that didn't work out. Now he try again up
north in Whitehorse in an all-Native place where they do real
good to deal with the issues facing these young Native people.
I know he'll come out right this time. I singing my song for
him and he seems to be taking it into him.

Mum, he says – and he hardly ever calls me Mum, usually
it's Lydie – Mum, are you disappointed in me?

Never I tell him. Never would I be disappointed in my

boy who stuck by my side through all the years. My baby boy who came back to me. Now it's time for my boy to go out on his own and do something to heal himself. It's time.

I feel guilty leaving you, he says.

Don't, I tell him. Never feel guilty; it's a waste of your energy. There are so many other things to feel. And this old lady's a tough bird, you know.

Jonah hugs me tight and hands over a little tin to me, saying he won't be needing it anymore, I'm to get rid of it. I know what's hiding in the little tin and later I will wash the stuff down the toilet with the poop, where it belongs with all the bad old memories.

Jonah slings his big green hockey bag over his shoulder and climbs on his bike. Waves to me as I stand on the front porch before he goes off down the street to where I can't see him no more. My old heart hurts for a minute. I remember when Mitchell went away too. But I have to think strong mummy-thoughts or I'll cry. I just hope it doesn't rain on my baby boy – it's a long drive overnight and all day up to the Yukon.

I go in to wash the dishes Jonah left in the sink from his breakfast. After the water stops running and the dishtowel stops squeaking on the plates, this old house is very quiet. I walk around the kitchen, then the living room, then in my room and finally in Jonah's room. I guess the bathroom's feeling left out, so I go in there and sit on the side of the tub for a while. If someone was peeking through my window, they would probably think this is a crazy old lady, living by herself and walking circles around her house. But if they knew what

I been through in my life and how I was born and where I was made to go to school and how I lost my children and how I fought my way back, then they wouldn't think I was crazy. They would understand why I have to walk around my house in circles. But it's okay – I'm ready to sit down now. *Wheel of Fortune* is on.

Sylvia comes by later and joins me to watch television. She makes some popcorn for herself – not for me, I have dentures – and makes some tea for both of us.

Why do you watch these dumb shows, she wants to know. She's always teasing me about these things I watch. I tell her the best part is watching the wheel spin and trying to guess where it's going to land. She says that makes her dizzy.

Jonah left I tell her.

Sylvia's head is down and to the side so I can't really see her face. She is too quiet. But then I hear her gasp a little like she having trouble breathing. She wipes her eyes with her sleeves, no makeup on them today.

He told me what happened, I say.

Sylvia looks up alarmed, like she might be in trouble, then she looks mad, confused. She run her hands through her hair very fast.

Only because he wanted me to tell you that he doesn't want you to get hurt. And because he want me to give you this.

I hand Sylvia a letter that Jonah wrote for her on some of my old flowery paper. She reads it quietly to herself, then looks up at me. She nods and reads it out loud for me.

Sylvia,
Have to go up to the Yukon for help with my drinking
problem, Hope you aren't mad about it. Never wanted
you to get hurt so I guess leaving you behind is my way of
making sure you don't. That doesn't sound like it makes sense
but I have to do this on my own to get better. It's not fair
to take you or anyone down with me on that journey. This
hurting has been going on for a long time, got something to
do with not knowing who I'm supposed to be – being taken
away from my family and my people when I was way too
young. It does something to a person that's hard to come back
from. Hope you still think of me as someone you would call
a friend. I just need time to learn how to feel and cry again,
because this old stone face ain't good for no one the way it is.

Take care of yourself,
Jonah

Sylvia is quiet and thoughtful for a while. Then she frown and say, it doesn't take Jonah to drag her down, she does it enough herself lately. But she understands what he must do. She says she will always want to be his friend.

I tell her I understand how she hurt. I understand that she is finishing up a whole part of her life in university and endings are always hard to deal with for sensitive people. And she is one of those people who feels things very deeply and very strongly.

Sylvia tells me how she doesn't know where to go next, what to do. She say she doesn't even really know who she is anymore, or maybe never even did.

Listen to me girl, I tell her. You are a wonderful girl with smarts and a good heart. Put those two things together and you'll figure out what you're supposed to do.

Lydie, she asks me, were you abused in residential school? She say she learn in classes all about what went on at Choutla School in Carcross and wondered what I went through there.

Yes, I tell her, yes. I went through all the bad stuff there. The physical, sexual, emotional abuse – it was all there. Not any of us escaped from it. One way or another, we was all hurt by those schools. I remember the young ones – I was older when I went – but I remember the young ones in bed their first nights there at the school, crying out for their mummies, but of course their mummies was far, far away and was crying out probably just as hard because they couldn't go to their babies. And those memories keep hurting years later. And I know that my own boys, when they was taken away to foster homes and reform schools, cried out for their mummy, and me knowing it and not being able to come to them made me go crazy from grief.

My Sylvie girl is crying hard now.

How do you live with the pain she wants to know.

You don't. The pain lives with you, I tell her. It's real big at first and takes up a lot of room around and beside you, keeping others away, but over the years it shrinks down and you can eventually fit it into your pocket. When you are old enough, and enough years have gone by, you can even scrunch it down into a little ball, like gum, and chew it down and swallow it into your throat. Once down in your belly, the stomach does its thing to churn it up and eat it. Then you know what happens to the waste – down the chute and left behind in the potty. But like bananas or pork chops, a little of it stays behind in your body. Some people exercise it away, some people throw it up, some people drink beers or take pills to make it numb. It makes some people grow real fat, real thin, or real red in the face, or maybe even shaky or stuttering on their words. The leftover ca-ca can cause some to lose the way they talk altogether, or change how they look, or forget who they used to be. But not me. No not me.

I was a lucky one. Because my mum taught me a little trick when I was real young. She gave me a song in the Tagish language – the language of her mother's people – and she put that song real deep down inside me so I never forget the words or the tune. She put it right down in there with the little round red things that run through your blood. So it's all wrapped around inside my body, to keep me safe over all the years of my growing, having babies, being a mother, losing my babies, them coming home again, leaving again, and now an old lady. And even though my mum died and her spirit gone to the spirit world and her bones and ashes are at the spirit house up in the Yukon, she is still here with me, after all the years, in the song. We was so poor, but that song she gave me was more important than any riches or money in the world.

All through my life I tell all the mummies I know to give such a song to their babies. Then, years later into the future, when the baby is being hurt – because everybody be's hurt – or even dying – 'cause everyone dies – and mummy can't be there, her words of love will still be there. Then no baby would die alone.

I hold my baby girl tight in my arms. She drownded in the river when she fell out of the canoe, no one knows why – she just tumble right on out. She was just one year old. I wasn't there when she died. I was on the shore. But I could see my Gracie underwater, I saw her little arms reaching out for the boat, the land, for something, for Mummy. But I was on the shore. Some men jumped in to save her but the current was too strong. She wash away down the river, like the little salmon. And I was on the shore.

I hold my baby, Sylvie, in my arms and rock her back and forth, rub her back. She cry and cry till she has no more tears and she gasping for air and calmness. Then, I sing her the song. The song my mummy gave me. The song we sung over Quiet Lake.

CHAPTER TWENTY-NINE
Miriam

Floyd was supposed to rotate the tires on this heap of Detroit metal but, of course, he never got around to it. It's pulling to the one side and rain has started falling since I left Calgary forty minutes ago. I'm heading back to Medicine Hat after a shopping stint in the big city with my sister. Blanche was her usual chatty self. She knows it all: child-rearing, cooking, traffic etiquette, even an expert on European countries, though she's never been to Europe. Or out of Alberta, for that matter. But she's good in a sisterly way. She never brings up the bad stuff of the past, and that's the only type of person I can stand to be around these days.

The sky looks as though it might form a tornado, dark and low. As I drive further into the thick of it, the rain increases in intensity. The sky is nasty gray and very menacing, much like my current state of mind. My vision becomes more and more hampered by the pelting rain on the windshield. I had been looking forward to clothes shopping with Blanche, but wasn't able to find anything I liked, so the trip hardly seems worth it now. Especially with the weather that's hitting me. Just my goddamn luck.

In behind a couple of eighteen-wheelers, the spray-back from the big truck directly in front of me is so forceful that my windshield wipers can't keep up. I allow the car to fall back a little, but a couple of SUVs go flying past me on the left because I am going too slow for them. The spray from these vehicles is jolting, and it's hard for me to keep the car straight. Seems like I have no choice but to overtake the big rig. I signal and pull up on the left lane, accelerating and holding my breath because I can barely see two feet in front of the car in the pounding rain. But something is wrong because all of a sudden the big rig is zooming off in another direction – or is it me? My car is rotating around, spinning, – must be hydroplaning. I watch as the big truck disappears, then everything is upside down. My head hits the car ceiling, hard. I can feel metal through my hair. Then down onto the steering wheel. I bite through my tongue. Then upside down, almost in slow motion, hitting the ceiling again. My head hurts from the first time. Finally the car thuds to a sudden stop on all four wheels. My body jerks to a stop with it. But my head is still spinning round and round. Steam is rising, and I feel rain on my face. I taste blood in my mouth. The windshield is smashed in.

My breath is ragged, forced; something is wrong with my lungs. I can't get enough air. I hold a hand up to my mouth and I see that it is cut jagged and covered in blood. Shaking, I am shaking all over. *I am still alive, aren't I?* But now what? I try to turn to my side to undo the seatbelt but a searing pain jolts a gasp out of me and sends me straight back into my former slumped-over position. I can barely move – the pain is excruciating. *Maybe I didn't survive this after all.*

"Are you okay, can you hear me? Ma'am?" A man's voice is coming from somewhere behind my head.

"Me? I can hear you – I just can't move."

"Yeah, you're pinned in there pretty good. I sent someone to call for help. Just stay still until paramedics can get here. It's important that you try to stay still."

I can't quite see the man – only barely in my peripheral vision – because I cannot turn my head. Also, the rain is falling in my face and blurring my eyes. I can't quite focus them.

"Can you stay with me?" I ask. "I think I'm hurt bad."

"Don't worry, I won't leave you – I'm a volunteer fire fighter. I'll make sure you're alright. What's your name?"

"Miriam Hardy." I can barely say my name. Everything is fuzzy. My voice sounds like a garbled drunk's. *Is that blood seeping out of my mouth?*

"Nice to meet you, Miriam. I'm Randy."

"Do you think I'll die, Randy?"

"You'll have some scrapes and bruises, but I think you'll make it through."

"But I can't feel my legs and there is so much pain in my abdomen. And my hand is all bloody." *Bloody, Bloody, Bloody* – the word rolls around like a pinball in my skull.

"Are you married? Can I call your husband?" Randy asks.

"My husband? Pierre, he probably wouldn't answer, it's

been so long." Pierre's face, his rugged features, devouring eyes, float in front of me, as though he was here holding my hand, and not some stranger. He should be here with me. Why did he leave me so long ago? Why would he choose to do that? Didn't he still feel the passion that we had? Or was it too much for him? But wait – we weren't ever married. Then there was Floyd. I never married him either. But he calls me his wife.

"I'm too injured to survive this. I can't possibly…"

"Don't think about that stuff, focus on something positive – your family, kids – you got kids?"

My head is spinning, exploding, all at once, foggy, fuzzy. I feel nauseous.

"Miss? Miriam? Did you hear me? Do you have kids?"

"I used to."

"They all grown up?"

"No. I don't know."

"Miriam, when is your birthday? Do you know what day it is today?"

"No, I mean I don't know them anymore. I had kids once. Little kids. Three of them. But not anymore. One I lost. Lost him right out of the front yard. And never saw him again. Do you know what it's like to lose a child?"

"Miriam?"

"They found his bones – up in the Badlands. What a place to find bones, huh? The Badlands. Funny thing is he used to love dinosaurs. Everything in his room was dinosaurs and we'd say, 'Tommy, what sound does a dinosaur make?' and he'd go nee-hee-hee-hee – like a horsey noise because that's what he thought dinosaurs did. And he could have been right, eh? I mean we don't really know what sounds dinosaurs made. Anyway, he was two years old when they took him. And killed him. And Tommy never got to see the dinosaur car – like on the Flintstones – I was keeping it for him in the closet for Christmas. I never got to kiss him again. Just looked at his bones. Up at the RCMP crime lab in Edmonton. They let me look at his little bones."

"Miriam, that's horrible. Downright tragic. I am so, so sorry."

"Yeah me too. That day they took him was the worst day of my life. But the day they found his little bones in a shallow grave up in the Badlands was the day I stopped being a mother to my other two. I had to. Because I couldn't survive it. I couldn't hardly survive it once, and I could never go through it again – losing another child. So I just stopped being a mother. Just stopped on that day. Just stopped altogether."

"It's okay Miriam, it's okay." Randy has his arm through the broken window now and around my shoulders. I am shuddering from…the cold? Rain? Shock?

"So here I am. And I should be dead right?"

"Don't say that, Miriam. It's not up to you to decide."

"No, but I should be right? When that happens to you, and your insides are ripped out from grief, you should just die right away. Not go on. Because in a sense they killed me too, when they killed my Tommy. Huey understood it. Boxcar Huey understood how you die like that. So please just let me go."

"Miriam, I hear the sirens from the ambulances. They'll be here any minute. Hang on, Miriam! Hang in there. Hold on to my hand. You are still alive."

I must have passed out. Because now I am dreaming. I am with my three children in a large garage – an airplane hanger, perhaps – on an island. We are waiting to catch a plane, one of those small floatplanes. It is pulling up to a dock inside the hanger. But there is only enough room in the plane for one child. I tell Sylvia to get on, but she cries and says she won't leave me, and she clings to me with her head buried in my neck. I hold her tight and whisper some reassuring words to her but lose patience when she won't let go of me. I hear the engine of the floatplane roar to life and when I look up, I see that the crew has taken Tommy and they are pushing off and the plane is exiting the hanger, moving out onto the water. I run to the edge of the dock and watch it take off with my Tommy. I curse at Sylvia for taking my attention away from Tommy, allowing him to be taken without my knowing. I watch as the plane takes off from the water and heads toward the shore. But something wrong. The plane is having engine trouble. It sputters and spurts and lurches violently to one side. I see Tommy's little body beginning to tumble out. A crewmember tries to catch him, but can't reach in time – he throws a rope instead. Tommy's little hands catch the rope as he falls out. He is flung down and is now being dragged from the rope in mid-air. He is clinging to that rope with all his might. The plane has turned back toward the hanger in an attempt to bring him closer to land. Hang on Tommy, hang on, just a little longer…I see his face and the fright in his eyes. I run to the edge of the island jetty, as far as I can go on dry land, then I dive into the water and splash desperately in the direction of Tommy. I can swim, but Tommy can't. He is only two years old. I see his face, his eyes wide, so helpless. I watch in horror as his little hands slip off the rope and he falls down, down into the water. A great splash bubbles up, and then he is gone.

I paddle frantically to the foamy spot where he disappeared into the sea. He is down there somewhere, but he is fallen far beyond my reach. He could not have survived this. I am numb with pain. I hear a cry and a loud splash somewhere behind me. Sylvia has jumped in after me. "Mommy! Mommy!" she cries. She is coming in after me to rescue me. But she can't swim – I never taught her. I see her head bob up and down, her arms flail wildly, and then she goes under. She is gone too.

I lost two children that day, in the dream.

CHAPTER THIRTY
Mitchell

I call her up like I always do when I need to hear her voice. Sometimes I just hang up right after she answers. But today I'll say some words to her. I know she needs to hear my voice too, every once in a while.

The same old robotic recording kicks in: "Will you accept a collect call from a Matsqui Correctional Institution prisoner?"

"Oh yes! Yes! Mitchell! Mitchell!" Lydie squawks into the phone.

"Hey there, Old Lady, got a dime for a man doing time?"

"What that mean? You need more money, my boy?"

"No Ma, it's just a saying is all." I chuckle. "Hey," I tell her, "I got the T-shirt you sent." A bright green shirt embroidered on the front with the words:

I AM THE SON OF A GROOVY OCTOGENARIAN.

I had to go to the prison library to look up the word "octogenarian." Turns out it means old person in her eighties. "Thanks for that, Ma. How is life at the homestead going?"

"Oh everything here is fine. Jonah is doing good too. I will graduate from the University of British Columbia soon," Lydie says proudly.

"I know, I been thinking about you and what present to get you."

"Ohhh…a present?"

"Nothing fancy. Kind of limited options in here. But maybe something from the woodworking shop. I been thinking maybe a chair – you need a chair?"

"That would be really wonderful Mitchell! Then every time I sat in the chair you give me, I would think of you – like your arms wrapped around me!"

Lydie's words punch a hole right in the center of my heart. I have to pause a moment to catch my breath.

"Yeah, well then, a chair it is. It'll take me some time. But I'll get 'er to you."

"I know you will, my boy. And I have some more wool socks to send to you – I made them myself."

Lydie has been sending me homemade things since I've been in here. She even sent me frilly curtains for the little window and a skirt to go around the sink in my cell. I keep these things folded up in a box high up on my top shelf. I need to know that they are there, but I can't look at them all the time. The pain it brings on is just too hard.

"Socks – that's great, Ma. I'll, uh, I'll be sure to wear them next winter."

That fist blocking my throat is throbbing. Words can hardly make their way out.

Lydie's voice flows into my weighted silence.

"I was just thinking the other day – about you when you were a little guy, and we used to make sock puppets, remember? We used to take Rooney's stinky old socks and sew buttons on for eyes? And you used to run around the cabin with it and make bear sounds. And it used to make me laugh so hard I would cry, remember?"

Tears force their way into my eyes. I blink them away, but they keep coming. I wish I could see her in person. But not here – not in prison.

"Mitchell?"

"Yeah, so?" I say through clenched teeth.

"I was just thinking about it, is all. You know how an old lady thinks about the past so much, all the good times."

She never thinks about the bad times. Damn her. Why can't I be more like that?

"Mitchell, my Mitchell boy – are you still there?"

"Yes, I'm still here." I wipe my face with my sleeve. "I'm sorry Mum...that I ended up here."

"Oh don't you feel sorry for anything. You hold your head high and proud and feel the strength of your ancestors there with you. You are never alone, you know that Mitchell? You are never alone."

"Mum, I love you."

"And I love you, my Mitchell. You go to sleep knowing that. And you never forget that you have a mummy who loves you. Always and forever."

CHAPTER THIRTY-ONE
Sylvia

Here she comes fresh off the plane from Toronto and whoosh-ing back into my life as if it had only been a month or so. But it's been a lot longer than that and I see that she has changed her hair color, again. She is unmistakeably Jessie, though, with her tall, self-conscious walk, pom-pom tuque bouncing off her head in the heat of early summer and her huge mis-chievous smile, eyes brighter than emeralds. She has a large, new designer bag and four more matching suitcases at the luggage carousel that we must lug through the airport. And she is only staying a month.

I graduate in two days' time and I wanted Jessie to be here to witness my convocation and to support me. She has a few more years to go in her quest to be an investigator of dead bodies, but she has wrangled a couple of weeks out of her summer break to spend with me. In the cab on the way to my place from the airport, she chatters on about Mom's recovery from the accident.

"How's Phil?" I ask her.

"Gone for the moment," she says. And on and on about how Phil decided he was going to take a job for a sports medicine company in New Zealand and he didn't even tell her he was considering it, just up and announced it one day and couldn't understand why she was a little upset at that.

"And so, are you still a couple?"

"Who knows," she says. "It's not a big deal, he's a goof anyway. Nothing to lose sleep over. Does it really matter?" She sounds like she's trying to convince herself that it doesn't. But I know she will figure things out. And be just fine. She always is.

"How is River, speaking of wayward b-friends?" she asks.

And on and on I go about the saga of River. The big break-up. The big confrontation at the bar. And naturally, the conversation leads to Jonah.

At home, I cook a wheat pasta dinner for Jessie and we talk into the night, trying to figure it all out.

In the morning, Mui comes in from a night out with Julie and brings in yesterday's mail with her.

"Look here, Sylvia, there's letter for you from Medicine Hat," Mui says. Jessie is closer and grabs the letter right out of Mui's hands.

"No way! It's Mom's handwriting!" Jessie screeches. I take the envelope slowly from her and look it over for clues as to what it might be, almost afraid to open it.

"Go on! Open the darn thing! I'm dying to see what she has to say to you," Jessie says, waving her hands around. "I'm surprised she could even write your address, with the way she's all bandaged up – like a mummy, the way Floyd describes it."

I slice open the envelope with my fingernail and find a card. On the outside are the words: *Congratulations on Your Graduation Day* with a picture of tall redwood trees in a forest, sun poking through the branches and twinkling on the lush boughs. Inside, in my mother's messy scrawl, were two little words: *Congrats – Mom.*

Jessie is speechless. But I am fascinated.

"This is weird, eh Jess? I mean, why would she pick a card like this? With this picture. Like a West-Coast rainforest. Is it symbolic? Maybe Floyd picked it – no – he's not capable of that, Mom would have had to pick it – maybe in the hospital gift shop. But I wonder why she picked this one and not some frilly floral one or…" I'm yammering on more to myself than anyone else.

"Who cares what card she picked!" Jessie says. "I'm just astonished that she sent you a card! After all these years of the silent treatment, now you get a graduation card in the mail! I bet it was the car accident! I bet she was going toward the light or something and she came back from it and saw the light!"

This afternoon I am taking Jessie over to meet Lydie. Lydie says she has a surprise for me too. When we get there, Lydie smiles and chats away with Jessie while I wonder why she's putting her coat on, as though we are about to go somewhere.

"Come, come," she tells us and we are off again on the bus. We end up at another bus station close to the city limits and Lydie buys tickets for us to go all the way out to Maple Ridge. She still won't tell me why. We head east and when we finally get there, Lydie has someone waiting for us at the bus station.

It is an old Native guy and he says little to me or my sister, but talks to Lydie in her language, or some language that she understands. He brings us to his old beater car and drives us through town and onto back-roads, past fields of berry crops and tree nurseries, on into rural parts where houses are sparse. We finally arrive at a rundown farmhouse, much like Lydie's little hovel except there are fields around it and feathers hanging over the front door. We enter at Lydie's urging and are greeted by a stiff-faced, very old Native woman.

"She is a medicine woman," Lydie tells me proudly. "That is your present."

"You gave me an old woman in Maple Ridge?" I hiss in Lydie's ear.

"No silly! She will work her medicine on you to help you heal from your sadness and confusion. That is my present to you."

Jessie looks at me with raised eyebrows and shrugs as we enter the dark little house. I can tell what she is thinking: *Why not? What would it hurt?*

"Okay, so what do I do? Is this like a séance?"

"No, no, come with me," the old medicine woman says. She takes my hand and leads me to a separate room and sits me down on a couch that must be nearly as old as she is. She has me lie down flat with no pillow under my head and shoos Lydie, Jessie, and the old man to the other room. When we are alone, the medicine woman begins singing and chanting in a language I cannot even begin to understand. She does this thing with smoke from burning cedar and waves it around my entire body. Then, she positions her shaky old hands just about an inch from my stomach and starts to slowly move them around in a circular pattern, saying some strange-sounding words as she does so. She repeats this for a good twenty or thirty minutes, then she stops.

"You can sit up now," she says. "It is over. The thing is gone."

"What thing?"

"It was like a serpent – a very big snake wrapped around your belly. Very tight. It was hard to get out of there. But I released it and it is gone now."

"There was a snake on my stomach?"

"A serpent creature. Wrapped very tightly, coiled like chains, choking off from the outside world, making an empty space inside that nothing could get into. It must have been there a very long time – since you were young – because it was in very deep."

I am speechless at her description. Then she summons Lydie and Jessie into the room and explains her diagnosis and treatment. Lydie is very happy to hear that the medicine woman was able to extricate the serpent from my belly. Jessie is slightly baffled.

"Did you feel anything?" she asks.

"Well, no, nothing painful. But actually...it does feel lighter in my abdomen. It does feel better, like maybe something was released."

"Maybe psychosomatic? Like some stress you were carrying around? Or maybe a tapeworm?"

"Now it's time for tea," Lydie informs us, cutting into our attempted rationalization of the healing session.

All the way back on the bus, Lydie keeps asking how I feel. "Different," I tell her. Something has definitely shifted.

That evening, the night before my graduation, Jessie, our Auntie Chris, Mui, and I went for dinner at a trendy eatery on 10th Avenue. Between the wood-fired pizzas and the Margaritas, we spun over the healing ceremony earlier that day and marvelled at what we could not understand or quantify. Then we started in on the card my mother sent and psychologized my poor mother into a neat little box. And that felt good because we could tuck forgiveness and understanding all around it. Being with Jessie, Mui, and Auntie Chris felt good too.

The night was warm and the sweetness of the spring blossoms was hanging in the humid air all around us as we sat on the outside patio. The wind was blowing in the right direction so we could smell the ocean. A good feeling took seed in the core of me, somewhere deep in my belly, somewhere which I guess was formerly confined and unreachable. I was glad my mom was going to be okay; I was glad my sister and my aunt were here with me. The excitement of the following day was building, and the future was wide open with whatever intriguing things life might bring next. The feeling kept growing and growing all night. The beginnings of a wonderful new life.

In the weeks ahead, that feeling would continue to grow until I would not be able to deny it anymore. One month after graduation, and a menstrual period missed, I would take the pee test, with Jessie waiting nervously and excitedly outside the bathroom door. And the test would come out positive.

But before all that, on the eve of my graduation, after dinner and a few non-alcoholic drinks, I lay down in my bed and fell into a deep, peaceful sleep. In my dreams, Tommy came to visit me. We walked together in a dewy green field picking flowers and blowing on dandelions. Not the flat fields, but the Cypress Hills, in east Alberta, rolling and undulating as though they are alive. We walked for a long time, then on into the luxurious, sun-dappled rainforest and tall beautiful redwoods. We stopped at a crystal clear stream and floated two little fluffy feathers down the creek. Tommy couldn't talk in sentences, but we could speak without words. He told me these two feathers would be waiting for me on the other side of the bridge when I went there. That was his present to me. Then I told him I had a present for him too. I took his little warm body onto my knee, reached my arms around him, and started strumming on my guitar, which I had found there in a thick tuft of ferns. I could feel his little heart beat and the gentle movements of his chest as his breath filled and then vacated his tiny lungs. He was so alive, I could feel him.

I started playing the guitar and singing a beautiful song that just came from somewhere deep within me. And how those words sounded, floating down that sparkling stream, in the redwood forest...it was amazing. And I sang and I sang, and Tommy clapped his chubby hands softly along with the beat, and he said, "More! More!" in his soft, baby way. When it was all done, his angel face was looking up at me smiling. That precious little face was filled with the infinite love of an innocent child and the sweet song that I gave him...Tommy's Song.

I'll never forget it.

CHAPTER THIRTY-TWO
Lydie

Heaving these old-lady legs over the rim of the bathtub is not as easy as it used to be. But I have to bath every couple of days or Mr. Stinky comes to visit. And especially I have to be squeaky clean today, because today is graduation day.

I fluff baby powder all over my body – silly stuff – only time you wear it is when you young or when you old – like diapers. My undergarments are next to go on and my big brassiere for these floppy boobies that fed all my hungry babies well. I bought some special stockings to hold in my varicose veins so I sit on my bed and roll these on – they are really thick and stiff, like in the olden days. Least I don't have to wear three more layers like at the Choutla School! I put some curlers in my hair – only for a few minutes –to get some soft waves. Then I put on some peachy rouge and coral lipstick, pretty, pretty. I wish I knew how to do up my eyes like Sylvia does, but that's a young-girl thing. Old women can't get away with that unless they looney-tooners. Then time for my dress, which is hanging all ready for me on the back of the closet door. It's in two parts, really. A skirt and a separate top but both same color – sky blue – so it looks like it could be a real long dress. A one-piece would be too hard to put on me these days. Because I'm not that bendy anymore. This dress is one of those wrinkle-free ones so I don't have to fuss with no ironing. I got it at a Weekenders Party I went to last winter at my cousin's house. Isobel – the one I be staying with and her two daughters when my lease is up here. Isobel only a few years younger than me and she went to Choutla School too, so we been good friends over the years. She be there today too in the audience.

My comfortable white shoes I strap on, and oh – but can't forget to put Doctor Scholl's pads for ladies inside! Long day ahead on my elderly feet. One more thing I can't forget. In my old jewelry box, under the satin lining on the bottom – the brooch that Jonah and Mitchell got me when they was just ten and twenty years old. It was for my birthday and that was a long, long time ago. And the metal is tarnished a little but I clean it here every once in a while because it means a lot to me. Mitchell told me that Jonah picked it out and they used Mitchell's money from his little job at the pool hall to pay for it. That wonderful trinket with the shiny beads and crystals sure meant a lot to me then, and even more today.

I fasten my clip-on pearl earrings and smile in the mirror. Dentures are clean and shiny too. I sneak a few raisins from my hidey drawer – not supposed to with my dentures – but those dried up little pellets remind me of my daddy. He used to buy me raisins from the store in Teslin for a treat. And today I know my daddy be with me. He be real proud of me – he always was. I ring up my cousin Isobel and tell her I am all ready, come get me. I sit on the couch, up straight, prim and proper, practising for later today. And I let one hand wander to the brooch and I touch it gently. It always makes me smile. How did those boys know it would?

On the campus, my cousin, her husband and my nieces (after hugs) have to go one way into the auditorium and me the other way, because I belong with the graduates on this day. They put us all together in a building behind the auditorium and give us black gowns to dress in with colored sashes depending on what kind of graduate we are. Some girls near me help me get the thing over my head and straighten it out on me. One missy has a pocket mirror and she holds it aways from me so I can see what I look like in the gown. Wow-wee! Looking good, old lady! Isobel will have to take lots of pictures of me in this fancy costume!

Next thing they do is line us all up in rows. Give the rows numbers, then call out the number and that row goes out the door and down the path to the auditorium. There are so many graduates this year that my row waits for a half hour to be called! Some staff people bring me a chair and water because I am the only old one in the row. Probably the oldest one in the entire room. Finally, they call the number to my row. We all straighten up and put smiles on our faces and march down the path and into the auditorium. Picture bulbs are flashing all around us as we walk in and take our seats. We wait some more to band music while the other rows come in. Once all the graduates for that degree are in there, the school president starts talking. And some other old white guys, deans and chancellors and stuff. And talk and talk and talk and talk. Why can't they make their speeches more interesting? They basically say the same thing, repeating each other, with no meaning, like politicians. Boring, boring, and more boring!

Then, it's time for us to line up next to the stage and get our diplomas and keep shuffling and shuffling like an assembly line. This isn't the way I thought it'd be. I thought it would be like the Oscar awards on television where we could go up and make a speech and thank everyone special to us. But no, probably there was too many of us. Now we are being herded on stage like cattle. I don't like this feeling. Grown-ups in suits, long black gowns, and straight faces moving us around, they call us up to take our place by our student numbers – just like at residential school. No, I don't like this one bit. Then the students have to go across the stage and kneel in front of the big fat white guy with the extra fancy gown on. He got the spiffy title of Chancellor. He supposed to tap us on the head to show that he allowing us to graduate. Then the graduates get a rolled-up piece of paper and walk off the stage. Most of the students bow down and kneel like they supposed to and the old white guy touch their hats. Some of the female students walk on by the white guy without kneeling – must be the feminists. That's what Sylvia said she would do. She graduated two hours earlier but she be in audience now she tell me. She be there to watch me. So I have to do this.

Finally, my turn. Up the stairs, smile big for the picture they take. Then across the stage to take my diploma and stop at the old white guy. He smile at me, I smile at him but I don't kneel down. I put out my hand and shake his and tell him, hello, my name is Lydie Jim. Then I move over to the announcer at the microphone and borrow the mic from him. He is surprised, real surprised. He step right back, not know what to do with an old lady taking over. I talk into the mic good and loud so everyone can hear me.

HELLO ALL YOU GRADUATES AND FAMILIES. I WAS JUST TELLING THE BIG GUY HERE THAT MY NAME IS LYDIE JIM. DON'T YOU THINK HE SHOULD KNOW WHO HE GRADUATING? I ALSO WANTED TO THANK THE NICE FOLKS OF THE GOVERNMENT AND THE UNIVERSITY OF BRITISH COLUMBIA AND ALL THE CORPORATE SPONSORS – SO MANY OF THEM I CAN'T REMEMBER THEM ALL – FOR LETTING ME GRADUATE WITH THIS FANCY PIECE OF PAPER. CAN'T FORGET TO THANK THE MUSQUEAM PEOPLE FOR THIS BEAUTIFUL LAND WHERE THE BIG SCHOOL STANDS – I NEED TO TELL YOU THAT MANY, MANY YEARS BEFORE UBC WAS BUILT, THE MUSQUEAM PEOPLE USED THIS LAND FOR LIVING AND TEACHING SINCE TIME BEFORE MEMORIES. LONG BEFORE ANY OF YOUR GRANDDADDIES WERE BORN OR EVEN YOUR GREAT, GREAT GRANDDADDIES. TO THE MUSQUEAM PEOPLE, THANK YOU, I COULD NOT HAVE GOTTEN THIS DEGREE WITHOUT WALKING ON THIS BEAUTIFUL LAND. BUT MOST IMPORTANT THING IS NOT THIS DEGREE. NO WAY. MOST IMPORTANT THING IS WHO YOU BE IN YOUR HEART. DOESN'T MATTER WHAT JOB YOU HAVE OR HOW MANY ALPHABETS YOU HAVE

AFTER YOUR NAME. GIVE LOVE AND BE KIND. PEOPLE WILL HURT YOU AND PEOPLE WILL TAKE FROM YOU. BUT YOU DON'T HAVE TO BE THAT TYPE OF PERSON. YOU GO BE THE PERSON WHO GIVES AND LOVES. THAT'S WHAT I HAVE TO SAY. THANK YOU FOR LISTENING.

Some people clap and holler, some laugh and some just stay quiet. I look out and though I can't see them – it's really packed tight in here – I know that Sylvia and my family are here for me. I know that my Jonah and Mitchell are far away but thinking of me right now. Even the dead ones are here with me on this day, my mummy, my daddy, my sister, and all my relations, on every day. Then Mumma comes to me with the song. As the clapping dies down, the song bubbles up to my mouth and out over the audience, silencing them and calming them, just as the waters over Quiet Lake did. The song I give to them.

CHAPTER THIRTY-THREE
The Priest and the Nurse

The young nurse picks up Father MacAvoy's patient chart to read the doctor's scrawls and the notes left by the last shift of nurses.

"...*has developed pneumonia...long-term neurologic sequelae...vertigo...severe brain damage...*"

The vertigo seems to be evident in his thrashing about and the need for his hands to be tied down. She watches as his head slowly moves from side to side, as if he is spinning round and round. His chest rises up so high that his back is not touching the bed – only his tethered arms keep him down. It looks as though he is drowning. People often think of comatose patients as lying perfectly still, like death. But in this line of work, she knows better. She'd only been doing it for a year but she had seen mothers kiss their children, lovers squeeze hands, words being spoken, all the while in a deep, undisturbed coma. The movement is frequently unintentional, robotic, involuntary, but sometimes it is real. She knows that.

"Just make sure he's comfortable," the head nurse had instructed her.

And she did, fluffing his pillows, wiping his face with a warm cloth, and draping him with heated blankets. He was so cold. Many drowning victims are that way immediately after a near-death experience. But his coldness continued on night after night on her shifts. It was as though he continued to drown all those days after the actual incident that had brought him here.

When people ask her what she does, she hesitates and ends up only telling them that she is a nurse. That is enough for most people. But some press on: "What kind of work do you do in nursing? What's your specialty?" She will tell them "palliative care" if they ask, but nothing more. To work with the dying is a special kind of work. Only a very few have the fortitude for it, because you are staring mortality in the face every day, be it with the very young dying of cancer, or the very old dying of Alzheimer's.

In the mornings, when she gets home from her night-shifts, she always enters her two-year-old daughter's room, like a watchful ghost. She crouches down at her crib and strokes her soft black hair. She watches her sleep in her peaceful innocence. Her daughter does not yet know what death is. She wishes we all could be kept in such a perpetual state of bliss. She kisses her daughter's forehead and goes to start breakfast.

Back on the nightshift – the witching hours, the nurses call it – she studies her paperwork for the evening while listening to the mumblings of the priest across the hall. It is the same sound she has been listening to for a month now. His demons just won't rest. They just won't let him go. From watching him, she believes that he has been drowning subconsciously for a month, in some type of agony that he will never be able to voice to another human being. Perhaps that is why he suffers so. Some unresolved issues that he never spoke of when he had the voice of life. But he is between life and death – closer to death, all the staff here know it. It is only a matter of time. *But how much more does he have to suffer?* the nurse wonders.

"I'm going down to the cafeteria for some pie. They've got lemon meringue today. Want me to bring you some?" the head nurse asks her.

"No thanks. You go on ahead."

"Keep an eye on that Father MacAvoy. I have a feeling that tonight is the night for him."

"Yeah, me too."

When the elevator doors close and the head nurse disappears, she walks across the hall to the priest's room.

"How are you this evening Father MacAvoy?" she asks him.

He is still, but she can see how his eyes are fluttering beneath his lids, and he moans softly. The nurse takes hold of his hand and strokes his aged skin. *I wonder what these hands have been through in almost a hundred years of life?* she wonders. *What have those eyes seen in all these years on earth?* His face looks very sad. His whole body undulates repeatedly beneath the blankets as though he were a fish trying to swim. She notices a small tear leak out from his eyelashes and dribble down his face. He is in pain on this earth.

She sits with him for ten minutes before getting up and walking over to the outlet where the breathing machines are plugged in. She kneels, and in one swift movement unplugs the powerbar to the cords. The machines fall silent. She walks back to the bed and strokes his thin hair.

"It is time to go now, Father. Just let go," she whispers.

Within minutes, he is completely still.

"The priest passed while you were down having your pie."

"Oh did he? I had a feeling. Thank you Gracie. I'll call the morgue porter."

"Actually, I tripped on the cord and — "

"Oh yes, don't worry about it. That happens from time to time. Doctors trip on the cords too. Can you sign-off on him dear?"

"Sure."

And she did: *Grace Athena Jim*

EPILOGUE
Jonah

Almost four years to the day that she graduated, Lydie died in her sleep. She called me just the other night to talk and we said our goodbyes for the last time. But she wasn't sad. Maybe she knew she was going – she was smart that way – but she didn't let on. Just told me how much I meant to her and that she loved me so much. Hearing that can make even a grown man cry. Now I have tears again.

Mitchell never got to say goodbye in person. I had to tell him on the phone yesterday and there was nothing but silence and unrelenting pain on the other end of the line. He meant to get out of prison and prove to Lydie that he could go straight, do something with his life, but I guess some part of him knew that she wouldn't live forever. He can't go to the funeral, of course, so he'll have to say his own private goodbyes within the walls of Matsqui. In another year or so, he'll be out; his time will all have been served. He tells me he plans on returning to the Yukon, to make amends with things in his past, and I can understand what he means. He'll be in his fifties by then. But it is never too late to start healing and to move on to a new phase of life. Mitchell will do okay, he's always been strong. After all, he's got half of Lydie in him.

Heading down the Alaska Highway from the Yukon now, I have a clearer vision of my life ahead of me and behind me. I am driving down to Vancouver to meet with family and Sylvia for Lydie's funeral. Isobel and some other cousins did all the arrangements, but it will be me and Sylvia who do the final part – with Lydie's bones and ashes. Being an elder like she was, Lydie requested that she be cremated like in the old days, but not grinded down. So her bones will still be intact. That was important to her, that her bones be left alone. She wanted us to have something other than dust to take up to the little spirit house in the Teslin cemetery where her ancestors' bones and ashes have all been laid to rest. That will be our job – me and Sylvia. To take Lydie home. It's been a long, long time since the old gal has been home. And it's finally time.

It will also be the babies' first time going home to where their relations come from. Sylvia convinced me to sell the bike and buy a car so we all can fit in there, kiddie seats and all. Lydie would have wanted the twins to take part in this too – she loved those little tykes more than anything. Oh how she fawned and fussed over them! You can imagine what a special grandmother she was to the twins. I only hope they can remember something of her. And Sylvia is a good mom – real good with the twins, real gentle and caring. Takes my breath away sometimes to watch her with them, how they look up to her, how they shine in her eyes. She named the boy Thomas and the girl Lydia. Tom-Tom and Lyds are over three years old now and they turned out more amazing than I could ever have hoped for. The day they were born was the happiest day of my life. Lots of people say that same thing, so it doesn't sound like it has much meaning. But it does. I never really knew what happy was until I saw their little fingers and toes, the color of their eyes. I worry that it won't last, this feeling. That it can't last because, like everything in life, there is an ending and usually it is a sad ending. But Lydie always told me not to worry about the ending. It was the happy parts in between to remember, and to live in those times like they were all that you knew.

I never thought it possible the first four decades of my life. Those two babies were the reason I went clean. Really went clean this time. You can't describe in words how you feel watching your little ones be born, take their first breath and learn to talk and walk. I wasn't there for it all the first time with my daughter. I couldn't be there for her. And I'll carry that sorrow and shame with me 'till the day I die. But I'm here now. Having the twins did something real powerful to me. Man, all these clichés. But there was some sort of shift; I could even feel it physically. Helped me come together after all the years of coming apart.

I'm away from them a lot – my babies and Sylvia – with my job up in Whitehorse. But I go down at least twice a month and Sylvia flies up sometimes with them too. They live in Gibsons now, the place where the twins were conceived. Sylvia started a little dress shop there after she graduated – so much for her psychology degree – but the shop really took off. She hand-sews some type of trendy dresses, hippy clothes I call them. She makes pretty good money from the tourists and from shipping her stuff around the country to other boutiques. She's got a little flat there on top of her store and it makes a nice home for her and the twins. And that feisty cat with the weird name she got from her old roommate. Comfortable, cozy little place and it smells like the baking she always does. When I go there, it's home for me too.

But my job is up here and my people are too. After finishing the treatment program, I enrolled in an addictions worker course at the college in Whitehorse. Before I even got my diploma and marked three years of sobriety, I had a job offer to work as a counselor. There's a huge demand for it up in northern communities. After a lot of counseling and many healing ceremonies, I now am able do home visits to help other people try to put their lives back on track. Who would of thought it four, five years ago – that I could do something like this, let alone be any good at it? There was a point in time when nobody wanted me in their houses. All those foster homes we Indian kids got shuttled through. Nobody wanted a raggedly little Indian kid with a track record of being bad and violent. And all those damn dreams, nightmares really, through the years about knocking on people's doors but never being able to go inside. Now I'm always knocking on doors to go in to many houses, homes, and the people there welcome me. Lots of places I just walk right in, don't even need to knock. They're happy to see me, my clients.

I know how it is for them. I know because I am one of them too – just on the other side of the clipboard these days. The system relegated so many of us to a life in the gutters.

There was no choice in the matter; no kid chooses to be a victim. And the feet kept trampling away up on top our heads, not even aware of what they were stomping down underneath. But a few of us made it out of the gutter, crawled up again to the sunlight. I was one of those few. And I want more to rise with me. It's not too late.

People tell me I make a difference in their lives; help them make changes; help them leave the bad stuff behind. So that's what keeps me up here, away from my babies and my Sylvia. The people up here need me. And I need them.

Sure miss my three in Gibsons though, miss 'em so much it hurts sometimes. We should all be together. That's the way it should be – not separated. So now, riding in my new car, I reach down and feel the little velvet box in my coat pocket and smile about what Sylvia might think of the ring inside. Not an expensive ring, but pretty and sparkly, like her. I'm going to ask her. I don't know if she'll say yes – we've had kind of a tumultuous history. Not sure what to do when she got pregnant, both of us scared and uncertain. Fights over my drinking and hurting her in the past. Disagreements over parenting, coming from different cultures. Getting clean is never easy – it's emotionally taxing and it's hard on the people who love you. Then the travel back and forth, the long distance, long separations. But we always come back to each other, like there is some invisible thread pulling us back. Sylvia has always been there for me. I was thinking she could maybe start a branch of her store up in the Yukon. Lots of touristy stuff there so hers would fit in. Besides, a lot of her revenue comes from shipping her stuff out to other parts of Canada. Maybe she'll be mad at me for asking that. Maybe she won't know what to do. Maybe her nose will twitch the way it does, and her eyes will fill up with tears. But she means a lot to me – her and the twins. So I'm gonna try.

Sylvia told me, not too long ago, that her reason for being was and is to be a mommy to those children. "Precious little hearts," she called them. She giggled wildly at her own silly phrase, but then she looked up at me and I could see in her eyes that she really did mean that she loved them more than anything, even though she could never find the proper words to tell it. How she's changed from the self-absorbed, mouthy little girl she was when I first met her. Her hair is longer now, usually pulled up thoughtlessly in a ponytail, its natural color a nice auburn red. And her face is older, fuller than it used to be. Her body changed too, when she became a mother, more matronly, but still beautiful. Everything changed about her. And I love her even more.

She said that if we were ever to lose one of our children, (because they were premature and real sick back when they first were born) she will die knowing that she gave every ounce of her being for them. It was a pretty clear sign to me that Sylvia had passed from being a child herself into being a mother. And there is something very powerful and profound about that transformation. As for me, I told her, my reason for being was to share in those gifts – Tom-Tom and Lyds – we made them together. And I love them so much. I can say that now. I can say it strong. I *can* be a father. I have learned so much from the wearing of time and the healing people around me. It's never going to be easy. It's never going to be fair. But there are people who need me.

So I'm gonna try.

ACKNOWLEDGMENTS

This novel was conceived in a dream I had one night a couple of years ago. A Native Elder, whom I had known in the 1990s while I was a student at the University of British Columbia, came to me in the dream. I modeled the character of Lydie after this woman who befriended me over a decade ago. Lydie was not the real name of the Yukon Elder I had known, but many of the stories she told me have made their way into this book. I don't know what became of her, or even if she is still alive. But I will be forever grateful to her for sharing her stories with me and teaching me so much in her gentle, teasing way.

Many of the characters in *Song Over Quiet Lake* were inspired by real people I have known throughout my life. Of course, the characters have been shaped and restyled in a fictional way so they will be unrecognizable to those who know me. There is one exception to this, however. The "sister character" – Jessie – was almost entirely duplicated from my real life sister, Allison Burns. (I'm sorry Al, I just couldn't resist. Hope that's okay.) I should also note that my sister was instrumental in assisting me with all the forensic anthropology and dead-body details.

I also owe my gratitude to my dear friends who have cheered me on and read and commented on earlier drafts of the manuscript: Nicole Marshall, Vivian Ikari, Sheena Brown, and Jill Foraker Alexander. Friends and family from Canada to Colorado have also helped to support and motivate me in the writing of this book. Thank you – you know who you are.

The editorial team at Second Story Press has my utmost respect and gratitude. A special thank you to managing editor Carolyn Jackson for her belief in the emotional strength of the story. I also have to thank Colin Thomas of Vancouver for his most excellent and thorough editing skills, as well as his guidance on "Vancouver Verisimilitude." Truly, a great group of people at Second Story Press.

I also have to acknowledge two very important sources I utilized during the research for this novel. *Stolen From Our Embrace: The Abduction of First Nations Children and the Restoration of Aboriginal Communities;* (1997) by Suzanne Fournier and Ernie Crey was an amazing source of information and personal histories from residential school survivors. The bravery of the voices in this book was incredibly inspiring for me.

Also, I relied heavily on the book *Life Lived Like a Story: Life Stories of Three Yukon Elders,* by Julie Cruikshank in collaboration with Angela Sidney, Kitty Smith & Annie Ned

(1990). This phenomenal collection of oral narratives from female Yukon Native Elders was critical in providing me with the details and background information to bring my novel to life.

I am also very grateful for the support and encouragement of my immediate family, most of all my mother, Frances Parcher Burns. My mom has been my constant editor, spell-checker, grammar coach, and marketing and PR director since my writing journey began. Thanks mom! I also have to thank my partner Lupe, my squishy rock who props me up through the best and worst of times. And loves me no matter what. (Even though he prefers cowboy books to my kind of writing.) Thanks to my dad, Robert E. Burns, for the Burns in me. I just can't get rid of it. And of course, thank you to my divine pipsqueak inspirations, (my kids) Noe and Tova.